The Other Mothers

Book 5

in the *Chop, Chop* Series

by
L.N. Cronk

Front Cover Photography by Peter Finnie.
Back Cover Photography by Brian Jackson.

Spanish translations provided by
Vicki Oliver Krueger and Jessica Gilway.

ISBN Number: 978-0982002773

Published by Rivulet Publishing
West Jefferson, NC, 28694, U.S.A.

For Vicki, Mimi and Halle,
mis hermanas en Cristo de la Escuela de Comunidad de Dos Ríos.

Blessed is the man who perseveres under trial, because when he has stood the test, he will receive the crown of life that God has promised to those who love him. - James 1:12

~ ~ ~

THE FIRST FULL week of spring had been a great one. On Tuesday, I'd finally gotten my cast off (I had broken my leg just before Christmas). Thursday, I'd gone to the YMCA during the day and done laps for the first time in over three months. Friday (yesterday), had been my twenty-ninth birthday and my wife, Laci, had made me a chocolate chip, peanut butter cake. And now? Now it was Saturday and I was at Cross Lake with Tanner, fishing for the first time since October.

For the past twenty minutes, we had been circling an island in his bass boat (his pontoon boat was still in dry dock). We were trolling along slowly, casting our lines toward the shore, when we neared a dock. As we drew closer, I noticed a real estate sign tacked to the front of it.

"Pull over there for a minute," I told Tanner. He guided the boat toward the dock and then let it coast. I looked up at the rough-hewn log cabin – it didn't appear that anyone was home.

"You should buy this for me," I suggested, pointing at the sign. "As a birthday present."

"You're the one with the big bucks, Mr. Engineer," he said. "I'm just a lowly P.E. teacher."

"I wonder how much it is?" I grabbed the dock.

"You in the market?" he laughed.

"Actually, I've been thinking about buying a place."

"You're kidding."

"No, I'm not."

He looked at me for a moment and then said, "Well, call 'em up. The phone number's right there."

"Now?"

"Why not?"

I couldn't think of a reason why not, so I pulled out my phone and dialed the number. After I'd described the property, the lady who had

1

answered the phone gave me a price.

"How much land is with it?" I asked.

"Two acres," she said. "And it has an excellent rental history. Are you looking for a vacation home or investment property or . . ."

"Just a weekend place," I told her.

"Well, if you'd like to see it, I'd be happy to show it to you. It's not occupied right now, so I can set up a showing just about any time you'd like."

"Okay," I said. "Thank you. I'll let you know."

"Well?" Tanner asked as I closed my phone.

"I don't know if it's a good deal or not," I said. "I haven't priced anything else."

"Wanna get out and look around?" he asked. "It doesn't look like there's anyone there."

"There's not," I agreed. "She said it's not occupied. Apparently it's a rental."

"That means it's been trashed."

"Really?"

"Do you take care of things when *you* rent them?" he asked.

"Yes."

"It's gonna be trashed," he said, tying off the boat.

We hopped onto the dock and walked up a stone path that led to the porch. The windows in the front were too high for us to see anything, so we walked around toward the back.

The back door had a window that looked into the kitchen and I pressed my face against it.

"Doesn't look trashed to me," I said. "Looks like stainless steel appliances and custom tile flooring."

"Let me see." He peered in.

We walked off the deck and around toward the other side. That's when we saw a little wooden door next to the stone fireplace.

"What's that?"

"I bet it's a woodbox," Tanner said. "You stack your wood out here and then just open this door and throw it inside right next to the fireplace."

He turned the piece of wood that was holding the door shut and pushed it open. We poked our heads into the opening and could see right into the living room.

"I can't believe it's not locked!" I exclaimed.

"I don't think people *lock* wood boxes."

"Well, they should," I argued. "Anybody could get in there."

"If somebody wants to get in there, they're just gonna break a window," Tanner said. "Locks are made for neighbors."

"If I bought it," I said, "I'd put a lock on it."

"Of course you would."

"The living room doesn't look trashed either," I said, looking inside again.

"Well, get in there and check it out!" Tanner said, giving me a push.

"No! We're not breaking in!"

"It's not *'breaking in'* if you don't break anything."

I looked at him doubtfully.

"You're thinking about buying it, right?"

"Maybe," I admitted.

"And she said you could see it any time you wanted, right?"

"Yeah, *when she's here with me!*"

"Oh, just get in there!" Tanner said. "This way if you're not interested you won't waste her time."

"And if I *am* interested then I'm gonna have to pretend I've never been in there before."

"I'm going in," Tanner said and he disappeared into the house. The next thing I heard was a long, low whistle.

"Wow!" he called.

I scrambled in after him and echoed his whistle. "Wow!" I repeated.

We looked around at the granite counter tops, maple cabinets and terracotta tile in the kitchen. In the living room there were hardwood floors, leather furniture and a stacked stone fireplace.

"Oh," Tanner said, looking out the front window. "You're gonna *love* this!"

"What?" I asked as I peeked into the dining room.

"Hot tub on the front deck," he said. "Overlooking the lake."

"No way," I said, heading toward him.

"Yes, way."

"Wow," I said again.

Tanner unlocked the door to the deck and walked out onto it.

"That real-estate chick's gonna get all this commission and *I'm* the one who showed it to you," he complained.

"I can get that friend of yours to be my agent," I suggested.

"Sierra?"

"Yeah."

"You're *really* thinking about buying this place?"

"Yeah."

"I'll call her," he promised.

After we'd looked around at all the rooms we crawled back out through the woodbox and closed it behind us. We walked all around the house and yard and then finally walked back down the stone walkway to the dock.

"It'd be pretty cool if you did buy it," Tanner said as he untied the boat. "I could leave my pontoon boat here and then I wouldn't have to pay a slip fee at the marina."

"I'd charge you more than the marina would."

"Not if I let you use it for free . . ."

"True," I agreed as I pushed us away from the dock.

"You think Laci's gonna go along with this?" he asked, starting the engine.

"Probably not at first," I admitted. "But I think I can convince her that it would be a good investment."

"Would it be?"

"I don't think the price of lakefront property goes down."

"I doubt it," he agreed.

"Maybe I could rent it before I make an offer," I mused. "Make sure it's what we want."

"That's a good idea."

"We could leave the kids with her parents next weekend and come up here for a couple of days."

"Why don't you wait until your anniversary?"

"That's a good idea," I said, "but I'm afraid somebody might snatch it up if I wait too long."

"Oh," Tanner said.

"I could tell her it's an early anniversary present though," I decided. "A nice, romantic weekend all to ourselves."

"Uh-huh." He gave me a little nod.

"I'll take her to Dante's," I said. "It's this really nice restaurant about fifteen minutes from the marina."

"I know."

"You've been there?"

He nodded.

"Oh. Well, anyway," I went on. "She loves to go there. It's her favorite place."

"I know."

"How would *you* know?"

"Because," he answered. "I used to take her there all the time when we were dating."

"In high school?" (They had gone to the prom together during our junior year . . . as *friends*.)

"No," he said, shaking his head. "In college."

I looked at him and didn't say anything. He tilted his head at me hesitantly.

"You . . . you *did* know that we dated in college?" he asked slowly.

5

"Didn't you?"

"Oh, sure," I nodded, waving my hand at him dismissively. "Of course I did."

He looked at me uncertainly.

"I did," I insisted, glancing away from him. "Laci doesn't keep secrets like that from me."

How could Laci keep a secret like that from me?

Somehow I managed to get through the rest of the trip – saying all the right things and nodding and joking and smiling. But I could barely bring myself to look Tanner in the eye again – it was all I could do to breathe.

I might not have known all the details about Tanner and Laci dating, but I knew enough to know that I had been lied to.

And I knew enough to be mad.

~ ~ ~

LACI AND I had started dating the summer before our junior year in high school, but after my best friend, Greg, and his father had died in the middle of our senior year, I had pushed her (and everybody else including Tanner) away. Laci and I had seen each other for about a year after that, but only as friends . . . only as two people sharing the greatest loss of their lives. And then – for the next three years – Laci and I hadn't seen each other at all. Hadn't even talked on the phone. Technically, I guess, Laci hadn't exactly been my girlfriend anymore.

But during those three years that we were apart I had dated no one – *no one*. And I'd never had any reason to think that Laci had dated anyone either. I'd always believed . . . no, not just believed – *known* – that Laci had trusted God to bring me back to her and that for those three long years she had waited patiently for me.

I'd always known this and believed this because Laci had always allowed me to know it and to believe it.

Why do you love me? I had asked her when we'd gotten back together.
Because God told me to.
When?
In preschool . . .

She had been obediently waiting for me ever since God had let her know – in preschool – that I was the one for her.

That's what she had told me.

~ ~ ~

WHEN WE FINALLY arrived back at Tanner's house, I said a hasty goodbye and jumped into my car. My mind was swirling as I drove home. I could barely see straight.   I pulled into the garage, went straight into the kitchen, and immediately saw Laci. She was standing at the window, watching the kids play in the backyard and she turned her head toward me as I entered. I stopped short and she looked at me for a very long moment.

"I'm sorry," she finally said in a quiet voice and I saw her eyes fill up with tears.

He had called her.

As soon as I had pulled out of his driveway, Tanner had *called* her and warned her that I knew.

Unbelievable.

"Well, this just keeps getting better and better, doesn't it?" I asked coldly, and I wheeled around and stormed back out the door, slamming it as hard as I could.

I got back into my car and pulled into the street, not sure where I was heading or what I was going to do when I got there. Before long, I found myself at the park and I pulled in, got out of my car, and started off on one of the walking trails.

I'd been on my feet a lot already during the day, and my leg was beginning to ache, but with the thoughts that were swimming through my mind, I barely noticed at all.

I didn't like the idea that Laci had dated *anyone* in college, but the thought of her with Tanner was almost more than I could bear. And not only had they dated in college, but Laci had lied to me about it. And now they were apparently conspiring with each other behind my back.

8

Could it get any worse?

Of course it could get worse. Laci could be on the phone with Tanner right now. I could see her – sobbing into the receiver – telling him what a jerk I was being and how sorry she was that she'd ever married me in the first place. I imagined her wondering if it was too late for her and Tanner to try again. The kids already thought of him as "Uncle Tanner" and they were young – how much of a stretch would it be for them to start calling him "Daddy"? He was probably on his way over to the house right now . . .

Suddenly I felt an overwhelming need to get back home. Despite the pain in my leg, I had traveled almost half of a mile. The loop I was on though was over three miles long and it was going to take me forever to get back to my car if I kept going. I turned around and headed back the way I'd come.

When I got back into my neighborhood and neared our driveway, I noticed that there were about five cars parked in front of the house. *That's* when I remembered my birthday party. I looked at Tanner's truck, parked alongside the curb, and shook my head, wondering how I was ever going to get through this. I sighed and headed reluctantly into the house.

As I walked into the living room, I was spotted immediately by Dorito and Amber.

Dorito (whose real name was Doroteo) was our only boy. He was eight years old and we had adopted him from an orphanage in Mexico where Laci had worked for several years. We'd known him ever since he was eighteen months old and had legally been his parents for over four years.

Amber was the same age as Dorito and was our foster child. Her mother had – until just recently – been in prison for driving under the influence. Amber's first foster home had been a nightmare, scarring her in more ways than one, and she'd coped with what had happened to her by losing the ability to speak. She used sign language to communicate, or – if she trusted someone enough – she would whisper into their ear. Amber had come to live with us three months earlier – right after I'd broken my leg. She was in counseling twice a week to help her deal with everything that had happened and she was making great strides, but I still couldn't wait for the first time that I would actually get to hear her voice.

The two of them ran across the living room to greet me, Dorito shouting "Happy Birthday!" over and over. They both threw their arms around me in exuberant hugs, but quickly recoiled.

"Ewwww!" Dorito cried. "You stink!"

Amber backed away, silently making a face.

"Sorry," I shrugged apologetically. I glanced around to my right and saw Tanner on the other side of the room. I had a feeling he was purposefully not looking my way, pretending instead to be engrossed in a conversation with Natalie, one of Laci's best friends.

"Was this a surprise party?" I heard my dad ask. I looked to my left and saw him standing next to Laci.

"No," she assured him.

"No," I agreed. "I just didn't realize how late it was."

"What's that smell?" Dorito asked.

"Fish."

"You went fishing without me?" he wailed.

"Sorry," I shrugged again.

I looked at Laci until she made eye contact.

"I'm going to go take a shower," I said. She gave me a tight nod and, avoiding looking in Tanner's direction, I headed up the stairs.

I took a quick shower, dried off and pulled on some pants and a t-shirt. Then I picked up my phone off of the dresser and called Laci, figuring that this would be more discrete than hollering down the stairs.

Dorito answered her phone.

"Hello?"

"Let me talk to Mom."

10

"Mom!" he called at the top of his voice so that I could hear him even through the closed bedroom door. "Daddy wants to talk to you."

So much for discrete.

"Hello?" I heard Laci ask.

"Can you come up here for a minute?"

There was a pause.

"I'll be right there," she finally said.

I was sitting on the bed, putting on my shoes when Laci opened the bedroom door and closed it behind her. She stood across the room, staring at me . . . waiting for me to talk. I could tell that she felt scared. Guilty. The look on her face let me know that she was desperate to make peace with me and was going to do whatever it took to make that happen.

"I know this isn't a good time for this," I said, nodding toward the door and the party that was going on downstairs without us, "but I need to know something right now."

She gave me a nod.

"And I want you to tell me the truth," I added.

She gave me another nod.

I took a deep breath and looked her right in the eye.

"How long did you date him?"

She thought for a minute and then answered, "A year and a half."

"A year and a half!?"

She nodded. That was longer than both of the times I'd dated her put together.

"Did you sleep with him?"

"NO!" she replied, instantly angry. "How could you even ask me that?!"

"This is *Tanner* we're talking about," I reminded her. She opened her mouth to argue, but then closed it again, silently conceding that Tanner wasn't exactly known for restraint and self-discipline in that department.

"It's *me* we're talking about too," she finally said quietly. "You know me better than that."

"I *thought* I knew you better than that," I said, "but I also never thought you'd lie to me."

"I didn't lie to you," she insisted.

"Why? Just because I never specifically asked you, *'So, Laci, did you and Tanner ever date while you were in college?'*. You think that just because you've never had to deny it means you haven't been lying to me?"

She didn't answer.

"It was a lie of omission," I told her and she looked down at her feet. A loud crash came from downstairs and we could hear Lily, our youngest child, begin to cry. Laci looked back up at me. I ignored Lily and said, "You should have told me."

She looked at me for a long moment and then nodded. We could still hear Lily wailing, but Laci didn't move. I knew she wanted to go to her, but that she was choosing me over Lily.

And I also knew that she was telling me the truth . . . she hadn't slept with Tanner.

"Go see what happened," I finally said, tipping my head toward the door.

"Are you sure?" Laci asked.

"Yeah," I nodded. "I'll be right down."

She looked at me hesitantly for a moment, but then turned and went out the door. I watched after her as she disappeared.

I still had a lot of questions. We were going to be up late that evening, talking deep into the night, arguing, justifying, explaining, pleading. Making up. Working things out. And there was no doubt in my mind that we were indeed going to work things out, but . . .

What if I'd found out that they'd slept together?

I was still staring at the doorway, into the empty hall when this thought came into my mind. The sounds of my birthday party and of Lily's quieting cries were drifting to me from downstairs.

Downstairs.

My whole life was downstairs: Laci, Dorito, Amber and Lily.

12

I asked myself again: *What if I'd found out that they had slept together?*

And then I answered myself with what I knew to be the truth: *We still would make up. We still would work things out.*

After all, what choice did I have?

It wasn't as if I could ever live without a single one of them.

~ ~ ~

THE FIRST THING I did when I got downstairs was to find Lily. Lily was four years old and had been adopted from the same orphanage that Dorito had been. Although she'd been born completely deaf, two years ago Lily had received cochlear implants and could now hear and talk. She didn't talk anywhere near as much as Dorito did, but then again, who did? I scooped her up.

"What were you crying for?" I asked.

She furrowed her brow and pointed at Laci's mom who was on her hands and knees, mopping something up off the kitchen floor.

"Uh-oh," Lily said, solemnly.

"Did you break something?" I asked her.

She nodded and stuck her lip out.

"Did you get hurt?"

She shook her head.

"Well, then," I said, kissing her cheek, "don't worry about it."

She glanced at her grandma one more time, but then gave me a smile. I kissed her again and put her down. I looked around for Tanner, but couldn't find him anywhere, so I found Laci instead.

"Where's Tanner?" I asked.

"He was gone by the time I got back down here," she said quietly.

I decided that was fine by me.

It was after ten o'clock by the time everyone had left and all the kids were in bed. I brushed my teeth and came out of the bathroom to find Laci sitting up in bed, waiting to start our inevitable discussion.

"Why didn't you tell me?" I began. "How could you keep something like that from me?"

"Well for one thing," she said quietly, "I knew you'd overreact."

14

"*Overreact?!*" I cried.

"Yes," she said calmly, as if I had just made her point for her exactly.

"That doesn't give you the right to lie to me about it for seven years."

"I didn't lie," she tried again.

"Semantics, Laci."

She sighed reluctantly.

"So you've kept this from me all this time just because you thought I was going to be mad?" I asked.

"Well, no," she hesitated. "That's not the only reason."

"What else?"

"It's not something I like to think about," she said finally, looking down at her hands which were in her lap, "much less *talk* about."

"Why not?" I asked, sitting by the foot of the bed. If this conversation was suddenly going to turn into a discussion about what a lousy boyfriend Tanner had been then I very much wanted to hear all about it.

"It was one of the worst times of my life," she went on.

"What did he do?" I asked with growing alarm.

"No, no," she said, shaking her head. "Not because of anything Tanner did . . . because of what *I* did."

"What did *you* do?"

"I don't even know where to start," she said, glancing up at me.

I sat quietly until she figured it out.

"It was really hard that first year after Greg died," she finally said, shaking her head, "but I always had hope. As awful as it was, I never really doubted that God was in control . . . that He had a plan. I wasn't real *happy* about His plan, mind you, but I still had complete faith that somehow He was going to work everything out for good."

"That's a whole lot better than I was doing," I muttered and she gave me a small smile.

"Even though Greg wasn't there to encourage me anymore," she said, "I could almost still hear his voice in my head, reminding me to be faithful to God and to trust Him and have patience and not to doubt Him.

"So even though you and I weren't dating anymore," she went on, "I believed that if I was patient enough, God was going to heal you and that we'd be together . . . just like He'd told me."

"And?"

"You completely stopped coming home," she answered.

"Oh."

"And once you were gone I started doubting Him. I doubted everything I'd ever believed and I felt so cut off from God. I've never felt so alone before in my entire life. It was one of the worst things I've ever experienced."

"And then what happened?" I asked when she didn't go on.

"Tanner helped me get through it."

"I'll just *bet* he did." I glowered at her.

"It wasn't like that."

"Let me guess," I said. "He was *there* for you."

"Yeah," she nodded. "He was there for me."

"That's the oldest trick in the book, Laci! Don't you know that? *Being there* for someone when they're on the rebound?! How long did he wait until he started going after you? Spring break?"

"He didn't . . . he didn't *'go after me'*."

"Right."

"He didn't, David. I went after him."

"You went after him?"

"Yes," she said quietly. "I needed a friend."

A friend?

"You were just friends?" I asked hopefully.

"No," she said even quieter.

"You were more than just friends?"

She nodded.

"How much more?"

"David—"

16

"How much more?" I asked again. "I wanna know. How much more?"

"I don't know," she said, throwing her hands into the air. "More! Okay? We were more than just friends."

"How far did you go with him?"

She rolled her eyes at me, crossed her arms, and leaned back against the headboard.

"I want to know what you did with him," I insisted.

"Nothing more than you ever did with *Samantha*," she said, angrily.

I thought about that for a minute. Laci knew everything about my relationship with my first girlfriend, Samantha. If she and Tanner hadn't done anything more than me and Sam . . . well, I guessed that wasn't *too* bad.

"That doesn't make any sense though," I told her, shaking my head. "Why would Tanner have gone out with you for a year and a half when his main reason for dating someone is-"

"It was different with me," she interrupted.

"Different?"

"He loved me," she said quietly.

"No, he didn't," I scoffed. "Tanner tells every girl he ever meets that so they'll jump into bed with him."

"No," she insisted. "He only said it to me."

"And you really believe that?" I asked doubtfully.

"I *know* that," she said softly, but with certainty. "He loved me."

And then she dropped her head. I couldn't see her face, but I knew she was crying. I didn't say anything for a moment.

"Did you love him?" I finally asked. She wouldn't look back up at me, but she nodded.

Earlier I had asked her if she'd slept with him, but it had never occurred to me to ask her if she'd loved him. Now that I had, I honestly didn't know which thought bothered me more.

"Why'd you break up?" I finally asked.

She looked back up at me with tears in her eyes. "God finally showed me that I wasn't following His will."

"And?"

"And we broke up."

I should have found a lot of comfort in the fact that God so clearly had a plan for my life, but instead I found myself angry.

"So, basically, if you'd done what you *wanted* to do instead of what God wanted you to do, you'd probably be married to Tanner right now instead of me."

"Don't do this, David."

"Do what?"

"Don't turn this into a pity party for yourself."

"A pity party?"

"Yes," she nodded. "No matter what happens, you somehow manage to only think about how it affects you!"

"I do not!"

"Yes, you do!" she argued. "Ever since you've found out about this, all you've done is feel sorry for yourself."

"Well excuse me for not liking the idea that maybe my wife would rather be with my best friend instead of with me!"

"Do you honestly believe that?" she cried. "These past seven years – everything we've been through – every way I've ever loved you? Do you honestly think that I've been secretly yearning for Tanner all that time?"

"I don't know," I said. "Have you?"

She stared at me in disbelief for a moment and then got up and stalked out of the room. I sighed and fell back onto the bed, staring up at the ceiling.

I laid there and thought about what Laci had said about me. After about ten minutes – in a rare moment of maturity – I actually wondered if she was right. Was I overreacting? Was I just feeling sorry for myself?

Possibly . . .

I got up off the bed and went to find Laci.

I went downstairs. She wasn't in the living room. The basement was dark. *Where could she be?* I worried for a brief moment, but then I had a sudden inspiration and headed back up the stairs.

Laci and I had been married for almost seven years and (I'm ashamed to say that) during that time, there had been plenty of nights when we'd gone to bed so angry at each other that we'd slept with our backs to one another, each of us hugging our own side of the bed so as to not touch the other. Sometimes one of us would wake up in the middle of the night to find that an arm or a leg had strayed over into the other's territory. We'd pull the wayward limb back to our own side and then struggle to fall back asleep, all the while reliving the row in our mind and justifying whatever it was that we might have said to the other.

The next morning we would only speak to each other in short, curt sentences ("Do you know where Dorito's gloves are?", "Is there any orange juice left?"), until finally one of us would attempt to make a joke. That would be the beginning of the end of our fight, and then – eventually – we would officially make up.

So I can't exactly say that Laci and I had never gone to bed mad at each other, but I *can* say that we'd never been so angry that one of us had decided to sleep on the couch in my office.

Now, however, that was exactly where I found Laci. She had pulled the sleeper sofa out of the couch and made it up with sheets, blankets and a pillow from the closet in my office. She was under the covers, her back to the door, pretending to be asleep.

"Laci."

She ignored me.

"Laci."

"What?" she finally answered, not turning toward me.

I sat down on the floor and rested my head on the bed. I felt like a dog.

"You know what I think?" I asked her.

"I can only imagine," she said dryly.

"I think that you love me very much."

She didn't say anything.

"And I think that I'm the luckiest man in the world and that I couldn't ask for anything more than what I've got."

She turned around and faced me.

"Who are you?" she asked. "And what have you done with my husband?"

"Really," I smiled. "You're the best wife anyone could ever ask for and I know that. And I know that you love me."

Her face softened.

"I've never wished I was with Tanner instead of you," she told me earnestly, propping herself up on her elbows.

"I know."

"I don't even let myself *think* about him like that," she went on.

"I know."

She smiled back at me, looking relieved.

"Do you let yourself think about *me* like that?" I asked her with what I hoped was a rakish grin.

"Occasionally," she smiled coyly.

"Oh, really?" I asked.

She nodded.

"Wanna tell me about it?" I asked.

She nodded again and I got up off the floor.

~ ~ ~

LATER, STILL ON the bed in my office, I lay with Laci's head on my shoulder. She was sound asleep, but I was wide awake, thinking about everything she had told me. Either Tanner had lied to her or Laci was quite possibly the only girl he had ever loved. I thought about that for a while. If he had loved her, how long had he loved her after they'd broken up?

Or did he still love her?

Oddly, the thought that he might still love her didn't bother me. I pressed my cheek to the top of her head. Laci was mine. She was always going to be mine. Every night she was going to curl up next to me and every morning she was going to wake up beside me. I thought how if Tanner ever did find someone to share his life with they would never compare to Laci. I turned my head and pressed my lips to her hair. She stirred slightly on my shoulder and I tightened my grip around her body.

I wondered how Tanner felt when he was around us. How did it feel for him to watch me put my hand on Laci's knee while we were eating dinner? How did it feel for him to watch me kiss her goodbye when he picked me up to go hunting? How had it felt for him to stand beside me in church as I had married her?

Maybe Tanner didn't care – maybe he'd never loved her. Or maybe he had loved her once, but had gotten over her a long, long time ago, never giving a second thought to the feelings he'd once had for her.

Maybe.

But somehow I doubted it . . . Laci wasn't someone you could get over easily.

And as I lay there with Laci in my arms, trying to fall asleep, I found myself feeling something for Tanner that I'd never experienced before.

I felt sorry for him.

21

I couldn't remember a time that I hadn't known Tanner. Like Laci, he'd always been a part of my life.

In every way Tanner was bigger than life. He was funny – always joking around – and had the sharpest wit of anybody I knew. He was smart, too. I may have always teased him about being a big, dumb jock, but both of us knew that it wasn't true. He'd been offered football scholarships to several universities including Notre Dame and Auburn, but had surprised everybody by accepting one from a less prestigious football school much closer to home.

Tanner was at least six and a half feet tall (more likely closer to six-seven). He was probably pushing two hundred and seventy pounds and every bit of it was muscle. During high school Tanner had been an all-star athlete, excelling in every sport he'd ever played. I'd lost count of how many times he'd been voted the MVP in one sport or another.

In football, Tanner would sometimes go for an entire game with only a break at halftime because he would play both defense and offense – defensive end, linebacker, tight end – whatever they'd needed. In basketball he'd averaged over twenty-five points per game and had erased over half of the existing school records. (He finished his high school basketball career with over two thousand points, seven hundred rebounds, and more than four hundred assists). In baseball, each of the three records he'd set (for most home runs in a season, highest number of no-hitters in a career, and most consecutive no-hitters) had stood for nine years – until his little brother, Jordan, had come along and shattered them all.

When we'd needed to pull up the carpet in our living room, Tanner had been there – hauling it off to the dump on a rented trailer that he'd hitched to his truck. He'd brought stones over and helped me put in a patio in the backyard. Last year on my birthday he'd spent the entire day helping my dad install my new hot tub with a deck around it.

I'd spent thousands of hours with Tanner – hunting, fishing, playing

22

racquetball and cards, skiing, shooting, swimming, lifting weights, canoeing, kayaking. We'd even tried sailing once. I could hardly remember a fun time in my life that Tanner hadn't been a part of – but now I didn't know if I would ever be able to face him again.

God, I prayed, *how am I ever going to get past this? You know I'm not good at this kind of thing. The thought of him kissing her, holding her, loving her . . . How am I ever going to look at Tanner again without thinking about that – without hating him? I'll try – I really will, but if I'm gonna be mature about this, too, then You're going to have to step in and help.*

I sighed and looked up at the dark ceiling and then turned onto my side, away from Laci, and gazed out the window. Light from the streetlamp outside reflected off of a bottle that was sitting on a table at the end of the couch. It was nail polish, and (although I couldn't really make it out in the dark), I knew that it was a little, clear bottle with pink hearts on it. Purple polish with silver glitter.

I picked it up and looked at it in the darkness, remembering how Amber had come into my office a few days ago, wearing a dress, her hair in curls and ribbons.

Look at you! I'd exclaimed. *You look gorgeous!*

She'd smiled and waved her purple fingernails at me.

Wow! You even painted your nails! Are you going to a fancy ball or something?

She'd shaken her head, giggled silently, and motioned for me to lean down so that she could whisper into my ear.

You're practicing? I'd asked and she'd nodded vigorously. *For what?*

She'd just grinned at me.

Oh! For the wedding? I'd guessed. Tanner's little brother, Jordan, and Greg's little sister, Charlotte, were getting married in six weeks. Amber and Lily were going to be flower girls.

She'd nodded again.

You're going to be a great flower girl, I'd promised her and she had beamed at me.

Now I twirled the little bottle in my hand. If it weren't for Tanner, that bottle wouldn't have been sitting there on the end table. Amber wouldn't have been sleeping in her room just down the hall. She'd be – well, I honestly don't know where she would be – but I knew that it wouldn't be here with me.

It was only because of Tanner that Amber had come into my office that day, waving her purple fingernails with silver sparkles at me. Only because of Tanner that I could tuck her into bed each night and listen to her whisper prayers into my ear. It was only because of Tanner that Amber was mine now. He had risked everything to get her out of that horrible foster home she'd been living in – his job, his freedom, even his life. He had done for her what I'd been unable to do.

I put the nail polish back on the end table and wondered how I had forgotten that for even one moment. It was then that I knew without a doubt that everything wasn't just going to be fine between me and Laci, but between me and Tanner as well. And right then I made up my mind that I was going to go over to his house in the morning and make sure of it.

I had no way of knowing it at the time, but it was one of the most important decisions that I would ever make in my life. One that I would be thankful for until the day I died.

~ ~ ~

IN THE MORNING I woke Amber up, had a talk with her, and then I showered and dressed. After we were ready to go I found Laci on the back deck, nursing a cup of coffee.

"Amber and I'll meet you at church," I told her.

She surveyed me and looked at her watch.

"Where are you going?"

"Out."

She eyed at me suspiciously. I walked over, leaned down and kissed her. She grabbed me by the front of my shirt.

"I love you," she said.

"I know," I smiled, kissing her again. "And I love you, too."

Amber came out onto the deck, her dress shoes clacking on the wood. She twirled around for us in her dress and I smiled at her too. Laci opened her arms and Amber walked forward for a hug.

"Where are you two going this early in the morning?" she asked.

Amber leaned in to Laci's ear and whispered something.

"Ah," Laci nodded. Then she looked at me in a knowing way. "Good luck."

At Tanner's I let Amber ring the doorbell. When he opened the door he surveyed the two of us and didn't say anything.

"Well, well, well," I said, raising an eyebrow at him. "If it isn't Casanova."

"If it isn't Pinocchio," he shot right back.

I couldn't help but smile. "Can we come in?" I asked.

He held the door open a bit more and Amber slipped in under his arm. I followed. We stood there in the living room, staring at each other.

"Here to invite me to church?" he finally asked.

"No," I said. "I don't want you at church with me."

"Phew." He wiped imaginary beads of sweat off his forehead.

"Tell him what you want, Amber," I urged her. She pointed at me. "No," I said, shaking my head. "*You* tell him."

Reluctantly she stepped toward him and motioned for him to lean down. He squatted down next to her and put a hand on her side.

"What do you want, young lady?"

She leaned forward and whispered in his ear.

He glanced up at me and raised an eyebrow.

"This was the best you could come up with?" he asked dubiously.

"Yep."

He smiled at Amber. "When do you want me to take you fishing?" he asked her.

She bent toward his ear again.

"Now?" he laughed. "I think you're going to church right now. Maybe we can go this afternoon. Or maybe next weekend. I'll talk to David and we'll figure something out, okay?"

She nodded and then leaned in and whispered one more time.

"In the back yard," Tanner answered when she'd finished. "Wanna go see him?"

Amber nodded and Tanner stood up. We headed to the back door to see TD – Tanner's dog.

Out on the back deck, TD wagged his tail furiously and wiggled his body as Amber giggled silently. Tanner picked up a well-chewed boat bumper and slung it to the far corner of his yard. TD took off after it like a shot and Amber went down the steps to take it from him when he came back with it.

"Give," Tanner ordered when Amber tried to take the bumper out of TD's mouth. TD obediently let go of the bumper and sat on his haunches, waiting expectantly for Amber to throw it for him again. She ran further into the yard, heaving the toy with all her might. TD bounded after it again, wagging his tail delightedly. We stood against the rail for a moment, silently watching them play.

"I didn't mean to start a fight between you two," Tanner finally said quietly.

I shook my head. "You didn't."

"I thought you knew," he went on.

"I should have."

"Don't be mad at her."

"I'm not mad," I said, turning my head toward him. "Don't worry about it. Everything's fine."

He shot me a doubtful glance.

"It is," I insisted. "Everything's fine."

"Good," he nodded.

We turned our gaze back to the yard and watched as Amber took the bumper from TD's mouth and threw it again.

"Laci thinks that you loved her," I said, glancing at him.

"She does, huh?" he asked, not looking at me.

"Yeah. She thinks she was different from *all* the other girls you've dated." I swept my hand across the back yard, indicating the vast expanse of females who had once called Tanner their boyfriend.

"Interesting," he said, still not turning his head my way.

"Did you?"

"Did I what?"

"Did you *love* her?" I asked, annoyed.

"What do you think?" he asked, finally looking at me.

I surveyed him carefully for a moment.

"I think Laci's different from all the other girls you've dated," I finally said, "and I think if you were ever going to fall in love with someone it could easily have been her, but . . ."

"But what?"

"But if you really did ever love her, I don't see how you could go back to just being friends with her after you broke up. And I don't see how you could stand being around me when I'm the one who married her."

"Interesting," he said again, turning his eyes once more to the back yard.

"So . . . did you?"

"Don't let him jump on you!" Tanner called to Amber. She nodded at him and pushed the dog away from her with her hand. TD sat down and waited for another throw.

"How's her counseling going?" Tanner asked.

"Don't change the subject!"

"Have they been able to give you any idea if she's going to start talking again?" he asked, ignoring me.

"Why can't you just answer me?" I asked impatiently. "Did you love her, or not?"

He was quiet for a long moment. "Does it really matter?" he finally asked, turning and looking at me again.

Now I looked away from him and settled my eyes on Amber.

Did it really make any difference?

"I guess not," I finally admitted.

Out of the corner of my eye I saw him nod.

"So," he said, turning his eyes back to the yard. "What's the counselor say about her talking again?"

"She said not to push it," I answered, giving up on trying to have a meaningful conversation with him. "We're just supposed to keep encouraging her to communicate however she's comfortable – whispering, signing, writing, whatever."

"Do you think she'll ever start talking again?"

"I don't know," I said. "I hope so."

At this moment Amber reached for TD's back and started scratching him above the base of his tail. He leaned into her, pushing his body against her. She plopped down on the ground.

"Amber! Don't get your dress dirty!" I called.

She turned and nodded at me. Then she stood up again and we

continued to watch her play for a few minutes.

"I don't know what I'd do without her," I said finally said, glancing over at Tanner. "I want you to know that I'm never going to take her for granted."

"Who are you talking about?" he asked quietly, still not looking at me.

I shrugged and returned my gaze to the back yard. "Take your pick.

~ ~ ~

AFTER CHURCH AND lunch, we returned home. I went into my office and searched online until I found a page from the real estate company I'd called yesterday detailing the cabin that Tanner and I had broken into. Laci was back out on the deck, enjoying the spring weather and watching the kids play when I shoved the printout in her face and announced, "Wanna see where we're going next weekend?"

"I didn't know we were going anywhere next weekend," she said, taking the paper from me and smiling.

"Just you and me," I told her. "We're leaving the kids with your mom and dad."

She looked at the paper for a minute and then smiled at me. "Okay," she said. "It sounds nice."

Laci was still feeling guilty enough about not telling me about her and Tanner that I knew she was going to go along with just about anything I suggested. I was not above taking advantage of this fact.

"I think I'm going to buy it," I said.

She looked at me, startled, and then finally said, *"What?"*

"It's for sale," I explained, sitting down in a chair facing her. "Tanner and I looked at it yesterday and I think it's a good price and it would make a great weekend place and I think I'm going to buy it."

"You can't . . . you can't just *buy it!*" Laci protested.

"Why not?"

"Well . . . well, because this is a huge decision and we need to think about it and talk about it first!"

"We are talking about it," I stated.

"I don't think this is a good idea," she said, shaking her head.

"Why not?"

"Well, first of all, that's a tremendous amount of money to be throwing away just so you can have a weekend place to go play at."

30

"I'm not throwing anything away," I said. "I could buy that place tomorrow and sell it in a year and probably make money. Mortgage rates are low right now and waterfront property is a great investment. Plus, we can rent it out when we're not using it."

"It's too risky," Laci argued. "If you want to make an investment you should buy some CD's or something."

"CD rates are low right now, too," I said. "CD's are a lousy investment. Right now it's a buyer's market, plus, that cabin has a great rental history. Besides that . . . I can't go fishing on a certificate of deposit."

She looked at me, dismayed.

"Look," I said. "We'll go there next weekend and you just see if you don't love it."

"I'm . . . I'm sure I'll love it, but . . ."

"But what?"

"I just . . . I don't think we should be buying any more property."

"Any more?" I asked. "The only property we own is this house."

"I know," she said. "I don't think we should get anything else."

"Why not?"

She bit her lip and looked at me hesitantly.

"What?" I asked.

She took a deep breath. "I guess maybe there's something else I haven't told you."

I raised my eyebrow at her.

"Does it involve Tanner . . . or Mike? Or any other man?"

"No," she laughed.

"Okay," I said, relaxing. "What is it?"

She hesitated for a moment before answering.

"Ergon offered me a job."

"A job," I said, flatly.

She nodded.

Ergon was Ergon Ministries – the organization that Laci had worked for in Mexico. They were a nonprofit that specialized in providing opportunities for youth groups in the United States and Canada to serve in the orphanage we'd adopted Dorito and Lily from and also in one of the nearby landfills. Ergon was the organization our youth group had worked with when we'd gone on our mission trip to Mexico the summer before our ninth grade year. It was on that trip that Laci had decided she wanted to spend the rest of her life working there. She'd gone on to get a bachelor's degree in – well . . . I don't know exactly what her degree was in – but it was in something that would qualify her to tromp around in a landfill and minister to poor children.

We had spent the first five years of our marriage living in Mexico. Then, three years ago, *thankfully*, we'd returned home to Cavendish. I had absolutely zero desire to ever set foot on Mexican soil again.

Just before Christmas, Ergon had flown Laci out to their headquarters in Texas to pick her brain and to draw from her experience and education. Or at least that's what I *thought* they'd flown her out there for. Apparently they had also flown her out there to offer her a job.

When Laci had come home from that trip it was a week before Christmas. That very evening I had broken my leg and spent the night in the hospital and the next night Amber was removed from her foster home. Then it was Christmas and right after that Charlotte had donated bone marrow to her newly-found half-brother and then suddenly Amber was placed with us and . . .

To say that a lot had been going on at the time would be an understatement. So, when I'd asked Laci how her trip went and all she'd said was, "Fine," I'd never really given it a second thought.

"What kind of a job?" I asked now.

"Pretty much the same thing," she replied, shrugging. "A bit more responsibility, better pay . . ."

She smiled at me and I glared back at her because she'd worked without pay for the whole four years we were there. This conversation was not about money.

32

"They begged you to come back, didn't they?" I asked.

"Kind of," she admitted.

"Did you want to?"

She nodded.

"But you didn't take it," I pointed out. "You didn't even mention it to me. You must not have wanted it too bad if you turned it down."

"I didn't exactly turn it down," she said. "It was kind of an open-ended offer. I can go back any time."

"And that's what you want," I stated, my voice flat again. She gave me the tiniest of nods.

I sighed and turned away from her, staring out into the backyard. Dorito and Amber were pulling handfuls of grass out of the freshly mowed lawn, making a pile of it on one of the swing seats for some reason. Lily was burying a doll in the sandbox.

Suddenly I had a thought and I turned back to Laci.

"What do you think God wants you to do?"

"I think He wants us to move to Mexico," she said softly.

I sighed again and stared into the backyard once more. "So why haven't you told me before now?" I finally asked.

"Because I know you don't want to go," she said.

"Since when does that matter?" I asked, not intending to sound as unpleasant as I did.

"It matters."

"When were you going to tell me?" I asked. "When the moving van pulled into the driveway?"

She was quiet for a moment.

"I asked God to be the One to make you realize that we needed to move," she finally said. "You know . . . I kind of asked Him to leave me out of it."

"You asked Him to leave you out of it?"

She nodded. "I asked Him that if He wants us to move to please convict you of it Himself so that it was *Him* telling you we needed to go,

33

not me."

"He hasn't convicted me of anything," I informed her.

"I know."

"I have no desire to move. He hasn't told me we need to move. We, we CAN'T move! How can we be Amber's foster parents if we move to Mexico?"

"I don't have all the answers," she admitted. "I just know that I asked God to work it out if He wants it to happen."

"And so you're perfectly content to stay right here until God convinces me that we need to leave?"

"Yes."

I turned to watch the kids again. Dorito and Amber had recruited Lily in their quest to fill the second swing seat up with grass.

"What are you thinking?" Laci asked after a minute.

"I'm thinking that as soon as God convinces me He wants us back in Mexico, you'll be the first to know."

"Don't push Him, David."

"I'm not pushing Him!" I insisted. "I'm just telling you that He has done absolutely *nothing* to make me feel like we should be thinking about moving back to Mexico. As soon as He does, I'll let you know."

"You need to pray about this and really try to listen to what He tells you," Laci warned.

"Don't worry," I assured her, watching Amber run beneath the maple tree for a fresh handful of grass. "If He talks to me, I promise I'll listen."

When I called the real estate office to make a reservation for the next weekend, I was told that they couldn't rent it to me.

"Why not?" I asked Mary Leah, the woman who had answered the phone this time.

"Well, sir," she said, "that property is under contract and the buyers stipulated that the sellers would only honor previously booked rental agreements. We're not allowed to make any new reservations."

"*It's under contract?*" I cried.

"Yes, sir."

"But I just called yesterday!" I exclaimed. "The lady I talked with yesterday didn't say anything about it being under contract!"

"You called about renting it?"

"No. I called about *buying* it! She offered to show it to me and everything. She didn't say it had already been sold!"

"Well, sir," Mary Leah said, "we're still showing the property to prospective buyers because the sellers are willing to accept backup offers."

"Backup offers?"

"Yes," Mary Leah explained. "A backup offer is an offer that is made after another offer has already been accepted. That way, if the original offer falls through for any reason, the sellers will have another contract to fall back on."

"Why would the other offer fall through?" I asked.

"Oh, lots of reasons," Mary Leah explained. "The buyers have a forty-five day opt-out period during which time they can get out of their contract for any reason."

"Does that happen a lot?"

"More than I wish."

"So," I clarified, "I can still make a backup offer and then if things don't work out with the first offer then I could buy it."

"Yes sir."

"Thank you," I said. "I'll be in touch."

I called Tanner's Realtor friend, Sierra, and made a backup offer on the cabin (much to Laci's dismay).

"Hey," I told her. "If God doesn't want us to get it, we won't get it, right?"

She looked at me uncertainly.

"Relax," I told her. "I promised you that I'm going to listen to what God says. I'm sure if He wants us to go to Mexico then He's going to make sure that I hear Him, loud and clear. Right?"

She nodded at me doubtfully, but didn't mention it again.

Of course the fact that the cabin I was so certain I couldn't live without was under contract was a clear sign from God that He wanted us to move back to Mexico . . . and naturally I ignored it. For some reason it seemed that whenever God had something in mind for me that wasn't in line with what *I* wanted, He always had to show me the hard way.

Is it really any great surprise that things were not going to be any different this time around?

~ ~ ~

EASTER WAS LATE in April this year. We were at church on the Thursday evening before (for the Maundy Thursday service) when I felt my phone vibrate. I stole a peak at it and saw that it was my boss, Scott, so I snuck out into the narthex to see what he wanted since he didn't usually call me in the evening unless it was important.

"What's up?"

"San Francisco's supposed to be particularly lovely this time of year," he said.

Part of my job as a structural engineer was to examine minimally affected buildings after an earthquake to assess how badly the structures had been damaged and to determine whether or not they were immediately safe for occupancy. I knew right away that there must have been an earthquake and that he needed me to be on one of the teams that was going.

"Now?" I asked. "Really?" (The kids had off from school all the way from tomorrow through the whole week after Easter.)

"Really."

"Do I get the pleasure of informing my wife about this," I asked him, "or are you going to tell her for me?"

"Sorry," he said.

I sighed.

"When?" I asked.

"You fly out tomorrow. Early afternoon. I sent you an email."

"Okay," I said. "Thanks."

When I got back into the sanctuary Laci looked at me questioningly.

Earthquake, I mouthed to her.

Her shoulders dropped, her mouth fell open in dismay, and then she tilted her head at me with an unhappy look her face. In a few seconds, when we stood up for a hymn, she leaned over Dorito's and Amber's heads toward my ear.

"You have *got* to be kidding me!" she whispered.

"Sorry!" I whispered back, hiding behind my hymnal. I glanced down at Amber, who was peering up at us curiously. I smiled at her and pointed to the correct words in the hymnal so that she could follow along – quite literally lip-syncing.

"The kids have got the next *ten* days off from school," Laci said as soon as the service was over, "and you're telling me you're not gonna be here?"

"Where are you going?" Dorito asked.

"There was an earthquake in California," I told him, tousling his hair.

"Awwww," he whined as we made it to the narthex. We shook hands with the minister and thanked him for the service and then Dorito and Amber and I stepped outside while Laci went to the nursery to get Lily. Amber, who had been holding my hand ever since we'd stood up to leave, tugged on my arm as we went through the door.

"I have to fly to California for a few days," I told her, already knowing what she wanted.

Why? she signed.

"For work," I said. "It's part of my job."

Amber looked worried and suddenly I felt it. She was unquestionably more attached to me than she was to Laci. She liked Laci fine – even told her every night that she loved her – but if she ever needed anything she always turned to me first. Amber and I – we had *bonded*. How well was she going to cope for one or two weeks without me?

She tugged my arm again I leaned down so that she could whisper in my ear. "I want to go with you."

"I'd love to have you go with me," I said, smiling at her as we walked toward the van, "but you can't."

Why?

"Because I have to work all day while I'm out there and there wouldn't be anyone to watch you."

Laci.

"No," I said. "Laci's staying here with you and Dorito and Lily."

Tug, tug. "We could *all* go," she whispered.

"No," I said again, shaking my head. "Dorito's got a tournament that starts Monday."

"You're gonna miss my tournament?" Dorito wailed.

"I'm really sorry, buddy," I said, unlocking the van.

He crossed his arms at me.

"Get in," I told him. I held Amber's door open for her. She was still holding my hand and she whispered in my ear again.

"Ask Mrs. White if she can come and take care of me," Amber begged before she climbed up into the van.

"No," I said, giving her seatbelt some slack so she could fasten it. "She's busy helping Jordan and Charlotte plan their wedding. Jordan's flying in tomorrow for the long weekend."

Tanner, she signed, ignoring her seatbelt.

"Yeah, right," I said, reaching across her and clicking the buckle together. "That's *not* gonna happen."

Why?

"Well, for one thing, because I don't think Tanner wants to spend his spring break babysitting you in San Francisco. For another thing, he probably wants to spend some time with Jordan."

I closed her door and saw that Lily and Laci had caught up with us.

"She wants to go with me," I told Laci, taking Lily from her. "Doesn't see why I can't just find someone who's willing to go to San Francisco with us to babysit her."

Laci laughed as I held her door open for her. Then I fastened Lily into her booster seat and went around to the driver's side. When I climbed in, Amber popped her head between me and Laci and cupped her hands around my ear again.

"Grandma Holland?" She was not about to give up.

I opened my mouth to argue with her, but couldn't think of a reason why that might not actually work. I glanced at Laci.

"What about my mom?" I repeated to her. Laci gave me a little shrug. I looked back at Amber and she put her hands together in a pleading gesture.

"I'll ask her," I told Amber, "but no promises. Now do your seatbelt back up."

I called Mom before I started the van.

"Hi, honey," she said. "Good timing – we just landed a little bit ago."

"Landed?"

"We're visiting your Aunt Cindy, remember?"

"Oh, yeah," I said. "I completely forgot you guys were going to New York. I guess that answers that question."

"What question?"

"I was calling to see if you wanted to go to San Francisco with me."

"When?"

"Like . . . tomorrow."

"Earthquake?"

"Yeah."

"Was it bad?"

"I don't think it was too devastating," I answered, "but I'm probably gonna be there for a while. Amber wanted to go with me but somebody's gotta watch her during the day and Laci can't go."

"Sorry."

"It's okay," I said as I started the van.

"I'd better go," she said, "Your father's getting annoyed."

"Because you keep bumping into people," I heard him say.

"Good luck," she said.

"Okay," I said. "Have fun. Tell Aunt Cindy I said 'Hi'."

We said goodbye and I backed out of my parking spot.

"Maybe my mom could do it," Laci suggested.

"Mmmm," I nodded, reluctantly.

"What?" she laughed. "My mom would be fun to go to San Francisco with!"

"Mmmm," I nodded again.

"You want me to call her?"

"I guess," I said, but then suddenly I was struck with a thought. "Hey! See if we can leave Dorito with her and your dad and *they* can take him to the tournament and stuff and you and Lily can come out there with me!"

"Mommy's not going to my tournament either?" Dorito cried.

"Dorito," I said. "Be quiet."

"You're going to leave me here all by myself?"

"Not all by yourself. You'd be with Grandma and Grandpa."

I could see him crossing his arms at me in the rearview mirror as Laci called her mother.

"Oh, wait," Laci said, closing her phone. "I just remembered. Mom's having that root thing done on her tooth Monday. They're gonna have to put her under and I said I'd drive her home afterwards because Dad's got some client flying in that day."

"She can't reschedule?"

"It's really been bothering her," Laci said. "I don't want to have to ask her to do that."

"I'm sorry," I told Amber, glancing at her in the mirror. She looked down at her lap, dejectedly. I must have looked dejected too because Laci mouthed at me, *She'll be fine*, and patted me on the arm.

"It wouldn't be fair if you got to go, anyway," I heard Dorito say to Amber, quietly.

"Dorito!" Laci admonished.

"Well, it wouldn't be!" Dorito said. "If I don't get to go, she shouldn't get to go!"

"Dorito," I said, "that is really rude. None of you are getting to go and it's all because *you* have a baseball tournament and Mommy has to stay here to take you to that."

"Sor-*ry*," he said, just as disrespectfully as he possibly could. "I'm just saying that it wouldn't be fair."

"That's it, young man," I said. "When we get home you're going straight to bed, and no TV or video games tomorrow."

"WHAT?" he cried.

"You heard me!"

"That's not fair!" he wailed. "I always get in trouble and she never does!"

"That's because she isn't *rude!*"

"Because she doesn't even say anything!" he exclaimed. "It's kinda hard to be rude when you don't talk!"

"Maybe you should think about giving that a try sometime," Laci suggested, looking back at him.

"I hope you're happy," I heard him say under his breath.

"This isn't Amber's fault," I told him, glancing at him in the mirror.

"So quit looking at her like that," Laci added.

In the mirror, I saw him turn his head defiantly toward the window, apparently making up his mind to quit before he got into more trouble. He didn't say another word.

"Don't forget you wanted to go by Tanner's," Laci reminded me. Tanner had wanted to borrow my dad's power washer to make good use of all his free time over spring break and it had been riding around in the back of our van for over a week.

"What?" Laci asked, turning to face Amber who was sitting directly behind her. (Apparently Amber had leaned forward and gotten her attention by tugging on her sleeve or tapping her on the shoulder.)

"Tanner?" Laci laughed. "You want to see if Tanner will go with you to San Francisco?"

I glanced back and saw Amber nodding. I looked at Laci and we smiled at each other.

"I already told you," I reminded her, "that there's *no way* Tanner's

42

going to want to go to San Francisco with us."

She reached for Laci again.

"She wants to know if she can ask him," Laci translated after she had turned to see what Amber wanted.

"Sure," I agreed. "You go right ahead and ask him, but I promise you that he's going to tell you 'No'."

"*San Francisco?!*" Tanner cried after we'd pulled up to his house and all of us had piled out of the van. He had come out to greet us and was now squatted down next to Amber, listening as she whispered in his ear.

"Where do you want this?" I asked him, hoisting the power washer out of the back of the van.

"Can I really go with you guys to San Francisco?"

I set the power washer down and stared at him, dumbfounded.

"Are you serious?"

"A free trip to San Francisco?" he asked. "Of course I'm serious!"

"Who said anything about free?"

Amber started jumping up and down, clapping her hands. Dorito crossed his arms tighter and managed to somehow look even more disgusted with his life.

"I don't know," Laci suddenly said, shaking her head and screwing up her face. "Is that really going to look appropriate for two grown men to go out there with an eight-year-old little girl?"

"It's *San Francisco!*" Tanner protested, standing up and putting his hand on Amber's shoulder. "Who's gonna care?"

"He's got a point," I told Laci. She still looked uncertain.

"David and I are gonna fit right in out there," Tanner assured her. He pursed his lips and blew a kiss in my direction.

"You know what?" I said, holding up my hand. "Forget it. I'd rather stay here and have my teeth pulled with Laci's mom."

Laci laughed.

"Can we go over the Golden Gate Bridge?" Tanner asked, walking to the fence that surrounded his back yard.

"Whatever," I said, picking up the power washer again.

"And I wanna ride the cable cars," he said, opening up the gate.

"You and Amber can ride cable cars all day long while I'm working," I promised as I set the power washer down inside the back yard.

"And then what?" he asked, winking at me knowingly. "What are we gonna do after that?"

I glared at him.

"I can't imagine going to San Francisco with someone as homophobic as you are," he laughed. "This is gonna be so fun."

"I'm not homophobic!" I exclaimed as we walked back to the driveway.

"Uh-huh."

"What's homophobic?" Dorito asked Tanner. His silent streak had lasted for about twelve minutes – a new, personal record.

"Thanks, Tanner," I said sarcastically. "That's really a conversation I wanted to have with him tonight."

"Your father," he told Dorito. "Your father is homophobic."

"I am not!"

"Right," he nodded. Then he raised his eyebrows at me seductively and said again, "This is gonna be so fun."

"Are you sure you really want to do this?" I asked him, seriously.

"Why not?" he shrugged. "I've got the whole week off anyway. It's perfect timing."

"We've gotta be at the airport by like, noon tomorrow. You gonna be able to get ready by then?"

"All I've gotta do is a couple loads of laundry and find someone to take care of the dog." We both turned and looked at Laci.

"Oh, lovely," she said, rolling her eyes. "Somehow my next ten days just managed to get *even better*."

44

~ ~ ~

LESS THAN TWENTY hours later our plane touched down at San Francisco International. On our way to get our luggage, Amber stopped me and motioned for me to lean down. She whispered in my ear, "I have to go to the bathroom."

"Well," I said, "you're just gonna have to wait. We'll be at the hotel in a little bit and you can go to the bathroom then."

She shook her head at me adamantly. I looked at Tanner in dismay.

"What's the problem?" he asked. "The kid can't go to the bathroom?"

"Laci always goes in there with her!" I exclaimed. "She can't go in there alone! What if something happens while she's in there?"

"David," he said, putting his hands on my shoulders and looking at me in mild disbelief. "She just has to go to the *bathroom*." (He shook my shoulders dramatically, in rhythm to the word *bath-room*.) "It will be *o-kay*." (*Shake, shake.*) "I'm confident that *some-how, some-way*," (*shake, shake, shake, shake*), "we can handle this."

"Do you know how many kids get abducted from public restrooms every year?" I asked quietly.

"How many?"

"Thousands."

"Uh-huh." He was done talking to me and he looked down at Amber. "Do you have to go to the bathroom, honey?"

She nodded at him.

"You're so lucky I'm here," he told her, taking her hand and leading her away. "Let's go."

I hurried after them until we arrived at a women's restroom. It was one of those huge deals with two separate entrances. Tanner knelt down next to her and pulled out his phone.

"Okay," he said. "Now, if you need anything, just push 'two' and then hit this green button, okay?"

She nodded and he had her practice. My phone rang.

"Who's number one?" I asked him.

"Laci."

I snatched the phone from Amber, pushed "1" and "send". It dialed his voicemail and he grinned at me. I shook my head at him and then unzipped Amber's fanny pack.

"If you call me," I told her, dropping the phone into her pack, "I'm coming in there. Understand?"

She nodded.

"And if you're not back out here in two and a half minutes, I'm coming in there. Understand?"

She nodded again.

"Don't forget to wash your hands," Tanner told her and she traipsed off.

After she was gone Tanner brought his watch up to his mouth.

"WhiteBoy," he said into his watch, "this is TanMan. We got a ten-thirteen. Over."

I smirked at him.

"WhiteBoy," he said again. "This is TanMan. I'm going to secure the other entrance. Be advised that you are instructed to maintain visual at all times. Over."

He wandered down to the other entrance and dropped his sunglasses onto his face. Then he leaned against the doorframe and crossed his arms, staring straight ahead. Periodically he brought his watch up to his mouth and pretended to talk into it. Eventually Amber came out at my entrance and Tanner rejoined us.

"WhiteBoy," he said into his watch one more time, "this is TanMan. Subject is secure. Mission has been successful. Over."

He looked down at Amber.

"You didn't drop my phone in the toilet, did you?" he asked. She shook her head and he held out his hand. She fished his phone out of her fanny pack and handed it back to him. Then he looked at me.

"Can we go get our luggage now," he asked, "or do you want me to sweep her for explosives?"

By the time we finally checked into the hotel room it was almost six o'clock. I had booked two rooms for the three of us. One room had two queen sized beds and was attached to a smaller room with a double bed. I took Amber's suitcase and put it in the smaller room. She watched me as I unpacked her things.

"Isn't this nice?" I asked. "You get a room all to yourself!" (At home she shared a room with Lily.) She pointed to the adjoining room.

"What?"

She kept pointing.

"That's where Tanner and I are gonna sleep. If you need anything, you can just come in there and get me."

She shook her head and pointed at herself. I sat down on her bed and patted the spot next to me. She scrambled up beside me.

"I know you don't usually sleep alone," I told her, "but I think you need to have a room to yourself."

She shook her head again and tears welled up in her eyes. After everything that had happened to her, I worried a lot that it would be very inappropriate for her to *not* have a room to herself. On the other hand, I couldn't stand to see her cry.

"How 'bout you start out in here so Tanner and I can watch TV after you've gone to bed," I suggested, "and then when we're ready to go to sleep Tanner can sleep in here and I'll take you in there."

She thought about it for a moment and then nodded. She jumped up, put her clothes back into her suitcase, zipped it up and looked at me expectantly, ready to go into the next room. I smiled at her and went next door where Tanner was hanging his shirts up in the closet.

"Pack up," I told him.

"Huh?"

"Pack up," I said, pointing to the small room. "You've got the single."

"Why?"

"Because you snore."

He looked at Amber and must have figured out what was going on.

"I'm being maligned," he told her. "I don't snore."

"And you lie," I added as he grabbed his shirts out of the closet.

We ate at a restaurant that was in the hotel and by the time we got back to our room, Amber was already rubbing her eyes. I had her brush her teeth and get her pajamas on and then I tucked her into bed.

"If you need me, just come get me. Okay?"

She nodded.

"Goodnight, sweetie," I said. "I love you."

"I love you, too," she whispered, and for the first time ever, she didn't make me put my ear near her mouth. She just whispered it into the air – almost like she was talking.

I smiled at her and kissed her forehead.

"Goodnight," I said again.

I closed the door when I left. Tanner was sitting on the bed that I would move Amber into later, watching a baseball game on TV.

"What are you two gonna do tomorrow?" I asked him as I sat down on my own bed.

Before he could answer, the door between our two rooms opened. We both looked at it and waited for Amber to appear, but she didn't. After a moment I got up and stuck my head in the room. She was in bed.

"Problems?" I asked.

She shook her head.

"Are you sure you're going to be able to go to sleep if the door's open?"

She nodded.

"Okay," I agreed. I walked back to my bed.

"Way to be firm," Tanner said, giving his fist a little pump into the air.

"It's not gonna hurt anything for her to have the door open," I argued. We were both keeping our voices low so she wouldn't hear us.

"No," he agreed, "but at some point she's going to have to *not* get what she wants. Things aren't always going to go her way."

"Things didn't go her way for a long time," I reminded him.

"I know."

"I just want her to have some happy times," I said. "You know?"

"Yeah," he nodded. "I know."

"So what are you going to do tomorrow?" I asked again.

"We're gonna walk across the bridge."

"I don't think that's a good idea," I said.

"Of course you don't."

"I'm serious," I said, quietly. "Did you know that it's the number one place in the world for people to commit suicide?"

"Yep," he nodded. "I was reading about it on the Internet last night. Number two is the Aokigahara forest in Japan."

"I don't want her to see someone committing suicide!"

He looked away from the television. "Do you honestly think people are lining up, waiting to jump and other people are just standing around watching?"

"It could happen."

"If I see any jumpers I'll cover her eyes," he promised.

"I'm also worried about how safe it is up there," I said.

"It's safe."

"How safe can it be if people can *jump* off it?"

He rolled his eyes at me.

"I'll tell you what," he said. "I'll wind her up real good in bubble wrap before we go. That way – if she falls – not only will she be well padded, but she'll float! And, if I wrap it around her eyes, she won't be able to see the jumpers."

"It's not funny, Tanner," I said.

He looked at me for a moment and then asked me in a serious tone, "If you don't trust me with her, why did you agree to let me come out here with you?"

I looked away and sighed quietly.

"It's not that I don't trust you," I said, looking back at him. "It's just that I worry about her."

"Really?" he said dryly, turning back to the TV. "I had no idea."

I was quiet for a minute.

"You know what I'm really worried about?" I finally asked.

"I can't imagine."

"This bathroom thing."

He rolled his eyes and shook his head.

"I'm serious, Tanner. It's not safe for her to be going into public restrooms all by herself. If she has a problem — if someone tries to hurt her or something — she can't even yell for help! What's she going to do? We didn't think all of this through before we brought her out here."

"I already thought about it," he said, leaning forward. "I'll find a woman — some woman with a little kid — that's going into the bathroom. I'll tell her what's going on and I'll ask her if she'll keep an eye on Amber while she's in there and I'll be standing right outside, waiting. Okay?"

I nodded, heartened that (even though he wouldn't admit it), he was worried about her too.

"I'll take care of her," he promised. "Trust me."

"Okay," I nodded again. "That's a good plan."

"It's an *excellent* plan," he said, sitting back and turning his eyes to the TV once more. "And if the woman I find happens to be *single*, well . . ."

"Single women with kids are the best," he went on, ignoring the fact that I was glowering at him. "Their biological clocks aren't ticking so much anymore so they aren't as likely to be pushing for a serious

50

relationship."

I stared at him hard until he finally looked at me.

"What?" he asked innocently, pointing toward the door that Amber had opened. "I've got my own room now – there's no sense in letting it go to waste!"

~ ~ ~

BY THE TIME I woke up in the morning, Tanner had already been to the fitness center, worked out, returned, showered, and was dressed. I jumped into the shower and dressed as well and – by the time I came out of the bathroom – Amber was up too and Tanner was brushing her hair.

"Okay," he said to her, pointing to the bathroom door. "Now get in there and get changed and then we'll braid it. Hurry up."

She scurried off to the bathroom with her clothes in her hands.

"You're going to braid her hair?"

"Of course."

"What do you know about braiding hair?" I cried. "You don't even *have* hair!"

"I have plenty of hair," he argued.

"You're *bald!*"

"I'm not bald! I just keep it short."

"Uh-huh."

"I do!" he insisted, pointing at his buzzed head. "This happens to be very intentional!"

"It's preemptive," I muttered.

"Why are you wearing a tie?" he asked, watching me working on it in the mirror and obviously trying to change the subject. "You're going to be crawling around in buildings that might fall down on you at any minute."

"Because I want to look good when they pull my body out of the rubble," I answered. (I didn't actually crawl around in buildings that "*might fall down on me at any minute*" – in the seven years I'd been doing this, I'd only gone into three or four buildings that I'd been in a pretty big hurry to get out of.)

"Really," he said. "Why do you have to wear a tie?"

"I don't *have* to wear a tie," I smiled, "I *get* to wear a tie."

"Are you serious? You don't have to wear one, but you do anyway?

52

What's *wrong* with you?"

"If you padded around in slippers and sweatpants all day, you'd welcome the chance to dress up a bit too. I even get to wear a fancy ID badge," I said, holding it up to show him. "It makes me feel so special!"

"Glad you're happy," he said, shaking his head. "You know she wants to come and see you when you're working, don't you?"

"I know," I nodded, giving the tie a final tug. "That'll last about five minutes once she sees how boring it is, but let me get down there today and check it out. I'll probably be able to work something out later in the week."

The bathroom door opened up and Amber stepped out, carrying her pajamas and wearing a bright orange top and blue jeans.

"I like that shirt," I said. "It'll be easy for Tanner to keep an eye on you."

Even Amber rolled her eyes at me.

"You ready to get your hair braided?" Tanner asked.

She nodded eagerly

"Well, get on over here then," he said, patting the bed next to him. "We'd better get started. It's been a while since I've done this – I'm out of practice."

"Of course the fact that you were ever *in practice*," I said, heading back to the bathroom to brush my teeth, "isn't concerning at all."

When I got back to the hotel room that evening at about five-thirty, Tanner and Amber were already there. Cartoons were playing quietly on the TV and Tanner was sitting on the couch with Amber next to him. She was leaning against him and he had his arm around her protectively. They were both sound asleep.

I was tired too and I debated lying down for a nap myself, but I was hungry more than I was tired, so instead I decided to wake them up. I knelt down in front of Amber and stroked her cheek with my finger. After a moment her eyelids fluttered open. She smiled at me.

"Hi, beautiful," I said.

"Hi," she whispered. Just like the night before, she didn't make me put my ear to her mouth to hear her.

"Did you have a good day?"

She nodded and Tanner stirred.

"What did you do?"

"We walked across the bridge," she whispered.

"You did?" I asked as Tanner opened his eyes.

"She slipped once," he said, stretching. "I barely caught her."

I glared at him and Amber giggled silently. I sat down on the other side of her and she stretched out her t-shirt so I could see it.

"I WALKED THE GOLDEN GATE BRIDGE," I read out loud.

She smiled proudly at me. "What else?" I asked, smiling back at her.

"I danced with a silver man," she whispered loud enough so that Tanner and I could both hear her.

"A *silver* man?" I asked, making sure I'd understood her correctly.

"Yep," said Tanner and Amber nodded. "He was silver."

"Like his clothes?"

"Like everything," Tanner said. "His clothes, his hair, his skin . . ."

(We didn't have silver people in Cavendish.)

"There were all kinds of street performers," he explained.

"On the bridge?"

"No," he said. "Pier 39."

"Oh," I said, looking at Amber. "And you got to dance with one of them?"

She nodded and smiled again. I smiled back at her.

"What's this?" I asked, pointing to part of a lanyard that I could see around her neck. She pulled the rest of it out from under her shirt and held it up to me – there was a plastic gadget attached to the end of it.

"What is it?"

54

Amber looked at Tanner worriedly.

"Go ahead," he urged. "Just do it for a second."

She looked slightly defeated but then grasped both ends of the contraption. She glanced at Tanner one more time and he nodded at her encouragingly. She looked back at me and then pulled her hands apart.

EARSPLITTING. PIERCING. DEAFENING.

How in the world that tiny, little thing made so much noise, I'll never know. It took about three seconds for Amber to put it back together so that it would shut-up and – in that time – I thought my eardrums were going to burst. After that it was quiet again (although my ears were still ringing) and I looked at Tanner with my mouth open.

"Personal alarm," he said, matter-of-factly.

"I LOVE it!" I exclaimed.

"I knew you would."

"You're a genius!"

"Yes. Can we go eat, now?"

"Absolutely. I'm buying."

"Yes," he agreed again. "You are."

"Come on," I grinned at Amber, taking her hand. "You even get to use the bathroom at the restaurant if you want."

~ ~ ~

THE NEXT MORNING Tanner pulled Amber's hair back into a ponytail.

"No braids today?" I asked wryly.

Amber shook her head with an impish grin on her face and Tanner gave me a suspicious smile.

"What are you up to?" I asked.

"Nothing," Tanner said, completely unconvincingly. Amber shook her head in agreement with him.

"Don't you dare get her hair cut!" I warned Tanner.

"I won't," he said, innocently.

"Where are you guys going today?"

"Back to Pier 39."

"You just went there yesterday," I pointed out.

"Yeah, but we didn't get there 'til the afternoon and we hardly had any time to do anything."

"What's there to do?"

"See the seals."

"What seals?"

"The *seals*," he said. "The famous Pier 39 seals?"

"Oh," I said. Then I asked, "Don't seals bite?"

"Oh, brother," he muttered.

"Don't you get close to any seals, young lady," I warned Amber, shaking a finger at her. She shook her head.

"So, why aren't we braiding our hair?" I tried again. Amber broke into another grin.

"Seals hate braids," Tanner said, straight-faced. "The attack rate goes way up when they see little girls with braids."

Amber's shoulders shook with soundless laughter

"You better not be getting her hair cut!" I warned him again.

56

"I'm not!"

"Laci will *kill* you if you cut her hair."

"I *won't!*" he said again.

I narrowed my eyes at him before I left.

"Don't," I said. "And don't let her get too close to the seals."

I honestly agonized all day about what Tanner had up his sleeve. *Was he going to get her a perm?* Doubtful . . . she already had pretty wavy hair and if they did that it was going to look like she'd stuck her finger in a socket. *Straightened?* Might not be too bad. *Colored?* Would Locks of Love take it if it was colored? Laci would be furious with Tanner if not. All day I worried about what I was going to find when I got back to the hotel.

When I arrived back at the room that evening, Tanner and Amber weren't there. I had talked to Tanner a few minutes earlier and knew that they were going to be back fairly soon, so I stretched out on my bed and closed my eyes. I dozed off, awakening to the sound of the hotel room door opening.

"Hey," I said, sitting up on my bed as Tanner held the door open for Amber. She stepped into the room and I saw immediately that her entire hand was wrapped up in a heavy gauze bandage.

"*What happened?*" I cried, jumping off the bed and rushing to her. I grabbed her shoulder with one hand and gently touched her bandage with the other. She looked as if she was going to burst into tears.

"What happened?" I asked again, looking up at Tanner.

"Seal bite," Tanner explained. "She lost three fingers."

I glowered at him and then looked back at Amber. She was now smiling, delightedly.

"Is there anything even wrong with your hand?" I asked her.

She shook her head and covered her mouth with her free hand, her shoulders shaking with laughter. It was then that I noticed the reason why Tanner hadn't braided her hair that morning.

Hair wraps. That's what I'd been worried about all day — hair wraps. She had three — each with a different charm dangling from it. One charm was of the bridge, one was of a cable car, and the third one was a seal.

"Did you get to see the seals?" I asked after she'd shown me each charm. She nodded as I started to unwind the fake bandage from around her hand.

"Was it fun?"

Another nod.

When I'd finished unwrapping her hand she pointed down and then held out a foot so I could see what else they had done. She was sporting a silver toe ring and a brand new pair of flip flops. The final touch was that they had *both* gotten henna tattoos, which (it turns out) are temporary. Amber's was of an octopus that was wrapped around her ankle and Tanner's was of a big, stupid scorpion on his big, stupid bicep.

Amber and Tanner both wanted to go back to Pier 39 for dinner that night. After we'd eaten, the three of us stood together and looked out across the Bay — the Golden Gate Bridge to our left. Amber was quietly working on an ice cream cone that I'd bought her when Tanner suddenly wrapped his arm around me and planted a big kiss on my cheek.

"Isn't this nice?" he asked, pulling me even closer. "You, me, the kid . . . all together, bonding?"

"Get away from me, you giant, perverted freak," I said, trying unsuccessfully to detach myself from him.

"Better be nice," he warned, squeezing hard and whispering in my ear, "or everyone will think we're having a lover's spat."

I rolled my eyes at him and tried to shrug him off of me again.

"I get custody of Amber if we break up," he said, finally dropping his arm.

"Fat chance."

Amber was still busily licking her ice cream cone. She didn't appear to be paying any attention to us. Tanner seemed to notice this too.

He crooked his finger for me to come closer.

"No," I said, shaking my head at him. "I don't think so."

"No, seriously," he said, and I could tell he wasn't going to kiss me again so I leaned toward him.

"She wants to go there," he whispered, pointing toward Alcatraz, which lay directly in front of us.

"Tonight?" I knew that ferries ran out there during the day, but I didn't think they had tours at night.

"No," he said. "Tomorrow."

"Why are we whispering?"

"I thought I'd better talk to you about it first," he said. "I didn't know if it was a good idea."

"Because of the ferries?"

"The ferries?"

"Yeah," I said. "You know. The ferries – capsizing, sinking, drowning . . ."

"What?" he cried. "No, not because of the *ferries!* You're a fairy!"

"Why then?"

"Because," he said, looking at me knowingly.

It took me a few seconds, but eventually I got it. Until just recently, her mother had been in prison. Was Alcatraz really the best place for Amber to go?

"Oh," I said.

"I didn't bring it up," he promised. "She asked about it."

I nodded.

"So, what do you think?" he asked.

"I dunno," I admitted. I stared at Alcatraz for a moment, watching its lighthouse flash at us.

"Hey, Amber?" I said after a minute, kneeling down next to her. "You know what that is?" I pointed at the island.

She nodded.

"Tell me," I said.

"The Rock," she whispered. I smiled at her.

"Yeah," I said. "It's real name is Alcatraz. Tanner says you want to take a ferry out there tomorrow?"

She nodded.

"Do you know what Alcatraz was?" I asked her.

She nodded again.

"What?"

"A prison," she whispered.

"Yeah," I agreed. "It was a prison."

She licked her ice cream.

"You know your mom used to be in prison, right?" I asked her gently. She bobbed her head up and down.

"Well, I'm worried that if you go out there that it's going to upset you – that you're going to worry that your mom was in a place like that."

She looked at me, steadily.

"Did you ever go see her when she was in prison?" I asked. Amber's social worker picked her up and took her to visit her mother about once a month now that she was out of prison, but I didn't know if she'd ever gone to visit her while she'd actually been *in* prison.

Amber nodded. *Lovely.*

"Well, then" I said, "if you go out there, you're going to see that this one's a lot different than the one your mom was in. This one is a lot older. Things are a lot better in prisons now than they were then." (*Weren't they?*)

She nibbled a piece of cone off of the edge.

"So if you go," I said, "you've got to remember that this isn't anything like where your mom was. Do you understand what I'm telling

60

you?"

She nodded again and I kissed her on the forehead.

"You can take her," I said, standing up. He looked at me and raised an eyebrow as I went on. "But I want her to wear a lifejacket on the ferry."

"I don't think they give you lifejackets on the ferry," he smiled.

"Well, then," I said, "just do the bubble wrap thing. That'll work."

"I got a tattoo," I told Laci when I called her that night.

"Henna?" she guessed right away.

"How'd you know?" I asked, dismayed.

"Because I know *you!*" she laughed.

"I could get a real tattoo."

"Uh-huh. Sure you could."

"I could," I mumbled. Mine was of a Celtic cross. Even though it wasn't permanent, I figured I might as well get something meaningful.

"How's Amber doing?" she asked.

"She's almost talking," I said.

"Really?"

"Yeah," I said. "I mean, she's still whispering, but it's louder and she doesn't make you lean down so she can do it in your ear. She's really doing great."

"Good," Laci said. I could tell she was smiling.

"How's the tournament going?"

"They're out."

"Already?!"

"Yep. Dorito did good though. He made a double play."

"Really?"

"Yep. I'll let him tell you about it, but my dad got the whole thing on video."

"Good!"

"I love you."

"I love you, too."

"I'll put Lily on while I go get Dorito."

"Okay. Goodnight."

"Goodnight."

Lily got on the phone.

"Hi, Daddy!"

"Hi, sweetie. How are you doing?"

"Good!"

"Good. Whatcha been doing?"

"Good."

"Mm."

"Dorito lost."

"Really?" I said.

"Uh-huh."

"Don't tell him!" I heard Dorito scolding her in the background. "I wanna tell him."

Lily began to wail as Dorito apparently took the phone from her.

"Hi, Daddy!" Dorito said.

"Did you take the phone from your sister?"

"Yes," he sighed.

"Put her back on."

"But *I* wanna tell you about my game!" he cried.

"Put her back on."

I finally heard a sniff on the other end of the line.

"Lily?"

"What?"

"I just wanted to say good night to you."

"Good night," she said, grumpily.

"I love you."

"Dorito took the phone," she complained.

"I know," I said, "but you've got it back now and I love you. Okay?"

62

"Okay."

"Do you love me, too?"

No answer.

"If you're nodding I can't see you," I reminded her.

"Yes," she said and I smiled.

"Good night, honey."

"Good night."

"Give the phone to Dorito."

After a moment Dorito came on the line.

"Hi, Daddy!"

"Hi, buddy. What's going on?"

"We lost."

"I'm sorry."

"But I made a double play!"

"Really?" I asked.

"Uh-huh!" he enthused, and then he went on to tell me all about it in excessive detail.

"That's awesome!" I said when he had *finally* finished. "I'm really proud of you. I wish I'd gotten to see it."

"Jordan was proud of me, too," Dorito said, and I could tell he was beaming.

"You saw Jordan?"

"Yeah," Dorito said. "He and Charlotte came to my game."

"That's great!"

"He's going to Hatiti."

"You mean, Tahiti?"

"Yeah. Jordan said if I keep doing good I can play in college like him one day."

"That's great, Dorito," I said. "I'm glad you did so good."

"Is Tanner there?"

"Sure. You wanna talk to him?"

"Yeah."

"Okay," I said. "Hang on."

I handed the phone to Tanner and watched as he held the phone up to his ear, barely able to get a word in edgewise as Dorito apparently relayed the entire game to Tanner, too.

"That's fantastic," Tanner finally said. "I can't wait to see the video. You wanna tell Amber about it?"

He paused to listen to Dorito's answer.

"Well, she's right here . . . I'm sure she'd like to hear about it."

Dorito must have decided that he was up for one more rendition because Tanner said goodnight to him and then asked Amber, "Do you want to talk to Dorito?"

She nodded.

"Okay," Tanner said. "Here he is."

She took the phone from Tanner and I watched her keenly because I'd never seen her try to talk on the phone before. Of course it turned out that Dorito did most of the talking and Amber only had to whisper back to him sporadically, ('yes', 'no', and 'uh-huh'). Tanner watched interestedly, too.

"You have a very unusual family," he observed as Amber nodded her head silently at the phone. "One kid who's deaf, one kid who doesn't talk-"

"And one kid," I finished for him, "who won't shut-up."

~ ~ ~

ON OUR THIRD full day there, at about three o'clock, there was an aftershock. I stepped into a doorway and called Tanner before the shaking had even stopped.

"That was *cool!*" Tanner answered the phone.

"Is Amber okay?" I asked.

"Aren't you worried about me?"

"No," I said. "Is Amber okay?"

"A big cinderblock fell on her head," he said. "I think she's dead."

Always a comedian.

"Where are you guys at?"

"Still at The Rock, waiting for our ferry."

"Did she do okay?"

"Yeah. She did great. I think she had a good time. Amber?" I heard him ask. "Are you having a good time?"

There was silence.

"I got a nod and two thumbs up," he reported. "Go back to your geeky job."

"Okay," I agreed. "See you tonight."

About an hour later, one of my team members tapped me on the shoulder.

"What's up?" I asked.

"We gotta fly," he said. "Got an emergency about four blocks away."

The emergency was at private aquarium/museum. An exhibit – Predator Reef – had started leaking as soon as the aftershock had hit.

"Thank you, thank you," the owner said, meeting us on the sidewalk in front of the building and shaking our hands. "I know it's safe . . . just need a green tag." What he needed was for us to certify that the building was safe for occupancy immediately so that workers could legally get in there without a huge liability risk and start transferring all of the fish into another tank before they were flopping around on the bottom gasping for water. He seemed pretty desperate. I disappeared inside before he could try to bribe me.

We did our inspection as quickly as we could, our boots sloshing more and more every time we walked past Predator Reef. Finally we were able go back outside and give the owner permission to send workers in.

"Move it!" he called to the workers who were standing by, waiting for their orders. Then he turned to the members of our team who were nearby and began handing us tickets. "Free admission," he said, "as soon as we're back in business."

"Thanks," I said, waving the tickets away, "but I live about seventeen hundred miles from here. I don't think I'm gonna make it."

"Oh," he said, sounding genuinely disappointed. "I wish there was some way I could thank you."

I smiled at him and turned to go, but then I suddenly stopped short. I wheeled around and faced him.

"You know," I said, "now that you mention it, there is something you could do . . ."

Tanner and Amber and I spent the evening with two pizzas, soft drinks and Buffalo wings, sitting on the "Authorized Personnel Only" access deck of Predator Reef. There were about six scuba divers below us in the tank. They were capturing sharks, saw fish, barracudas, piranhas and even crocodiles.

It was quite a show.

Every now and then – when something was brought up – one of the biologists would motion for Amber to come over and let her inspect one of the animals up close.

"There's just something about her, isn't there?" Tanner asked at one point, when she'd gone over to "pet" a sea turtle.

"Whatdaya mean?" I asked, dipping a wing into some blue cheese dressing.

"I mean, everybody's just enamored with her," he explained, waving his hand to indicate the two biologists who were squatted down next to her, talking to her intently.

"Kinda like we are?" I asked, ripping some meat off of a wing and smiling at him.

"I guess," he nodded seriously. "There's just something about her that . . ."

He looked at me as if unsure of what he was trying to say.

"There's something about her that makes you want to protect her," he finally said. "Something that makes you want to take care of her and make her happy. You know?"

"Yeah," I nodded, wiping my mouth with a napkin. "I noticed."

It was after nine by the time we got back to the hotel. I sent Amber into Tanner's room to change into her pajamas. She came out, instead, wearing her bathing suit.

"You aren't sleeping in that," I told her.

"I want to go swimming," she whispered.

"It's way too late," I said, shaking my head. "You can go tomorrow."

She put her hands together in a begging motion. I glanced at Tanner for help. Instead, he was standing with his arms crossed and a smirk on his face, watching to see if I could bring myself to deny her. I looked back at Amber who was still pleading with her hands.

"I guess," I finally conceded, "but just for a few minutes.

"You're so authoritative," Tanner said sarcastically as Amber ran into the bathroom to get a towel.

"Well," I said, sheepishly. "She's all inspired from watching the divers tonight."

"Right."

"Oh, like you'd be so good at telling her 'No'!" I snapped.

"I'd be better than you!" he insisted.

Amber came out of the bathroom with three towels. She handed one to me and tried to give one to Tanner.

"Oh, no," Tanner said, holding up his hands and backing away from the towel. "I'm zonked. I'm going to bed early tonight."

Amber's mouth dropped open in dismay.

"Tomorrow," Tanner promised. "I'll go with you tomorrow."

Amber's hands came together again in a pleading fashion again and then she tugged on his arm.

He glanced at me and started to say something, but then closed his mouth. He looked back down at Amber, who I think had managed to work up a few tears.

"Okay," he said, sighing heavily.

"Way to be authoritative," I smiled.

"The only reason I'm going," he said, not looking at me as he headed into his room to change, "is because I, too, was inspired by the divers."

Once at the pool Amber immediately climbed down the stairs into the shallow end and Tanner and I joined her.

After we'd splashed around for a few minutes and gotten thoroughly soaked, Tanner challenged me to a race.

"Just a few minutes ago you were 'zonked' and 'going to bed early'," I reminded him. "Now all of a sudden you wanna race?"

"The water has revived me," he explained.

"Um-hmm," I said. "This wouldn't have anything to do with the fact that you finally sense an opportunity to actually *beat* me, would it?"

"No," he said, defensively.

"I used to be on the swim team," I informed Amber. "Normally Tanner doesn't stand a chance against me."

"I let him win on a consistent basis," Tanner said slyly to her.

"But now that I'm so weak from being in a leg cast for three months and I'm barely able to *walk*," I went on, "he thinks that his chances of winning have greatly increased."

Amber smiled at both of us.

"Wanna race with us?" I asked her.

She shook her head.

"Why not?" I asked. "Come on! It'll be fun!"

But she just shook her head some more.

"Okay," I agreed, setting her up on the edge of the pool. "You can be our official judge. You decide who wins."

She nodded and smiled at me.

"Down and back?" Tanner asked.

"If that's all you're up to," I agreed and he made a face at me.

We started from the water because there were about thirty "No Diving" signs posted around the pool.

"On your mark. Get set. GO!"

After we swam down and back I popped up and looked around for Tanner, who was standing up at the same time.

"Who won?" we both asked Amber simultaneously. She pointed at Tanner with a sheepish smile on her face.

"Enjoy it while you can, big boy," I told him. "A few more weeks and you won't have a prayer."

"Ooooh," Tanner said. "I'm so scared."

"Wanna go again?" I asked. "Butterfly?"

He hesitated, but only for a moment.

"Sure," he said, and we took our marks again and went.

There's a technique to the butterfly, one that most people (including

Tanner) never bother to learn. But I had bothered to learn it – the butterfly was actually my specialty. When I finally touched the wall and popped up, my leg was aching, but I didn't need to ask Amber who'd won. Tanner hadn't even finished yet.

"That is such a *stupid* stroke," he complained, wiping water from his face, "I don't even know how it ever became an event."

"Ever heard the expression, 'sour grapes'?" I asked Amber.

She grinned at me.

"Underwater now," Tanner suggested. "We'll see who can go the furthest with one breath."

"Okay," I agreed. "But let me *catch* my breath first."

"What's the matter?" he asked. "Outta shape?"

"Yes, as a matter of fact, I am!" I cried. "That's what happens when you can't exercise for twelve weeks."

"Excuses, excuses," he muttered.

Amber hopped back into the pool.

"You gonna race with us this time?" Tanner asked her.

She shook her head.

"Why not?" I wanted to know. "I thought you wanted to go swimming so bad."

"I don't know how to swim," she whispered.

"*You what?*"

"I don't know how."

Tanner and I glanced at each other.

"You should learn!" Tanner said. "Do you want me to teach you?"

She nodded.

"I should be the one to teach her," I protested. "Not you!"

"How do you figure that?"

"Because I was on the swim team all through high school and college," I said, jabbing my thumb into my chest. "And I was a lifeguard."

"Big whoop," Tanner said, waving a hand at me dismissively. "I'm a *coach!* I spent four years learning how to train athletes."

70

"Yeah," I scoffed. "How many swim lessons have you given?"

"It's not about a particular sport," Tanner insisted. "It's about working with-"

He stopped in mid-sentence and we both turned suddenly to where Amber had been. She was underwater now, sitting on the bottom of the pool and gazing up at us while bubbles streamed out of her mouth. We each reached down and grabbed her, pulling her above the surface. She stood up and grinned at us.

"Never mind," Tanner said. "You can teach her."

"No way," I argued, shaking my head and wading away. "You're the coach."

The aftershock almost doubled the number of inspections my team was contracted for and Tanner had to fly home with Amber at the end of the week so they could both go back to school on Monday. I was going to have to stay in California for at least four more days without them.

"I'm going to miss you," I told Amber as I squatted down next to her before she and Tanner checked through security. "You be a good girl for Tanner and call me as soon as you get home, okay?"

"Okay," she whispered.

We hugged each other and I gave her a kiss on the forehead.

"I love you," I told her.

"I love you, too."

I stood up and Tanner looked at me expectantly.

"You're not getting a hug *or* a kiss," I informed him, reaching out my hand. He shook it and then pulled me into a hug anyway. It was a manly hug though – a football player-type hug with slaps on the back.

"Thanks for everything," I told him as we pulled apart.

"Glad to do it," he answered. "Anytime." And then he took Amber's hand and led her away.

~ ~ ~

IT WAS THE first week in May by the time I got back to Cavendish. When I arrived home, it was almost time for Jordan and Charlotte's wedding, which they were having as soon their spring terms were over in the middle of the month.

Almost a year earlier, Tanner and Jordan's middle brother, Chase, had been diagnosed with Huntington's disease. It was a devastating, genetic disorder that usually didn't show up until the victim was in their thirties or forties, but sometimes it could show up earlier – like it had with Chase.

Chase's diagnosis meant that Tanner and Jordan each had a fifty percent chance of having the disease themselves. When Tanner had found this out in the fall, he'd immediately decided to get tested and – *thank God* – had found out that he was clean. Jordan, on the other hand, had made the decision to not get tested. I guess he figured what was the point in getting tested since if he did have it, there was nothing that could be done?

The younger a patient is when they're diagnosed, the more aggressive the disease tends to be. This was certainly the case with Chase, who physically was doing so poorly that he refused to be a groomsman at Jordan's wedding.

Neither Tanner nor Jordan wanted Tanner to be a groomsman if Chase wasn't going to be one, and Charlotte didn't want bridesmaids if Jordan wasn't going to have groomsmen. Jordan and Charlotte, therefore, weren't going to have any attendants at their wedding.

But *I* was going to give Charlotte away (she had made me promise I wasn't going to cry). And Dorito was going to get to be the ring bearer. And Amber and Lily were going to be flower girls.

Our family was pretty special.

72

"What's Laci get to do?" Amber whispered in my ear at the rehearsal dinner.

"What's *Laci* get to do?" I asked loudly for Laci's benefit. "Nothin'. Laci gets to do *nothin'!*" I grinned at Laci and she rolled her eyes at me, shaking her head.

"Why do you get to walk Charlotte down the aisle?" Amber wanted to know.

"Well, usually the bride's father gives the bride away," I said more quietly. "But Charlotte's daddy died when she was a little girl and now she doesn't have anyone to give her away, so I get to do it."

Amber nodded and didn't ask any more questions until later that night, when I was tucking her into bed. It was then that she pulled my head close to hers.

"Are you my daddy?" she whispered.

Her question caught me off guard. This was risky stuff, but I answered without hesitating. "Yes."

"So," she whispered, "when I get married you'll walk me down the aisle like you're gonna walk Charlotte down the aisle?"

"Yes," I nodded. "I wouldn't miss it for the world."

She looked at me for a moment and then gave me a smile.

"You're gonna be a beautiful bride one day," I said. "I can't wait to see what you look like."

Her smile grew bigger.

"I love you," I told her.

"I love you, too," she whispered into the air.

I smiled back at her. "Good night."

"Good night."

The next day was the big day. I was worried that Amber might not have the courage to walk down the aisle in front of all those people, but it wound up being Lily who got stage fright and Amber had to take her by the hand and drag her to the front. Dorito got there way ahead of both of them, first trying to have a conversation with Jordan and then waving to Tanner, Laci and his grandparents while waiting for Amber and Lily to finally join him. Charlotte and I watched the whole thing from the vestibule by cracking the doors a bit and peeking through.

"They forgot to throw their rose petals," Charlotte said.

"You wanna call 'em back and have them go again?" I asked her. She shook her head, stepped back, and looked at me.

"You promised me you weren't going to cry," Charlotte said, accusingly.

"I'm not doing anything!" I exclaimed, throwing my hands up in the air (and I really wasn't, although I knew that if I tried to tell her how beautiful she looked, or how proud I was of her, or how much I loved her, I was going to be a mess).

"Are you ready?" she asked.

I nodded and she reached toward me.

"I love you," she said, pulling me into a hug. Then, into my ear, she said quietly, "My dad and Greg would be really glad that you're here for me."

"I thought you didn't want me to cry."

She pulled back and smiled at me and the music in the sanctuary changed to announce her arrival. The doors opened and I walked Charlotte down the aisle to where Jordan stood at the front of the sanctuary, waiting for her.

After the wedding we went into the fellowship hall for the reception. We were sitting down, eating, and Natalie was in the middle of telling us a

74

story about her father (who was suffering from Parkinson's), when Dorito interrupted.

"Amber and I want some more punch," he informed me, tugging on my tuxedo sleeve. I sighed heavily and Laci and I looked at each other.

"I'll go with 'em," Tanner offered, rising from his seat.

"No," I said. "You don't have to. I'll go."

"Naw," Tanner assured me, glancing at Natalie. "I've already heard this story." Natalie smiled at him and he took Amber's hand in one of his, put his other hand on Dorito's back, and steered them both toward the punch table.

"So, anyway," Natalie went on, "I get downstairs and Dad has completely wedged himself behind the hot water heater somehow. I still have no idea how he got back there, there's only about," she held her hands about eight inches apart from each other, "this much space between the tank and the wall."

"What happened?" Laci asked.

"Well, Mom and I tried for about five minutes to get him out of there, but it wasn't gonna happen, so pretty soon she's crying and wanting to call 911 . . ."

"What'd you do?" Laci asked.

"I called Tanner," she said, nodding toward the punch table. "He came over with this big step ladder and he drags it down into the basement and he sets it up so it's kind of straddling the pipes on the top, you know? It was just about impossible because it kept hitting the ceiling whenever he tried to lift it over the pipes, but finally he gets it over there and then he climbs up on our side and leans over so that he's reaching behind the hot water heater and-"

She was suddenly interrupted by a long, loud scream that pierced the fellowship hall. Lily looked at me, Laci and I looked at each other, and a hush fell across the room. Laci and I both stood up hurriedly.

"You stay here with Natalie," I heard Laci instruct Lily as I rushed away from the table. Laci was right on my heels.

75

When we arrived, Tanner was squatting down next to Amber who was holding an empty cup and still screaming. Dorito watched her with a frightened look on his face.

"I didn't mean to!" he said as soon as he saw Laci and me. Amber whirled around and looked up at me. The entire front of her white dress was completely covered in red punch.

"He RUINED IT!" she cried. "He RUINED my dress!"

"I didn't mean to!" Dorito insisted again.

Tears were pouring down Amber's face and I knelt down next to her and opened my arms. She stepped into them, still wailing, and threw her arms around me. She buried her face into my neck and I could feel hot tears against my skin. I could also feel cold punch from her dress soaking into my rented, white shirt.

"I looked so pretty," she sobbed against me.

"You're still so pretty," I whispered, wrapping my arms around her and standing up. "Laci can get it clean," I promised in her ear, "and if she can't we'll buy you a new one."

She continued to cry as I stood there with her in my arms, gently rocking her back and forth. My eyes found Tanner and then Laci. They both looked at me with something near shock on their faces and I knew I was looking back at them the same way. I closed my eyes and hugged Amber tighter and then I opened them and smiled at Laci and Tanner. They started smiling back at me and before long we were all grinning at each other like idiots.

It was the first time any of us had ever heard Amber speak.

~ ~ ~

FOR THE NEXT few days after that, Amber seemed to feel that the only time she needed to actually talk out loud was when she was mad at Dorito about something. By Tuesday afternoon they'd had three major arguments – one regarding whether or not you have to sell your houses and hotels before you can mortgage your property in Monopoly (you do), one about who was taller (I couldn't believe Dorito even bothered to argue with her about this since Amber clearly had at least six inches on him), and one about who the dog liked better (I honestly don't know who had the upper hand in that one). Every time we heard them quarrelling, Laci and I would smile at each other.

"How much longer do you think it's gonna be before we stop perceiving this as a great thing?" Laci asked me during the dog dispute.

"A good, long while," I smiled.

~ ~ ~

AMBER'S CASEWORKER, STACY Reed, was scheduled for a visit on Wednesday afternoon, the week after Jordan and Charlotte's wedding. I couldn't wait to tell her that Amber was finally talking, but (as it turned out) I didn't have a chance because she walked right in on their fourth argument: which one of them was going to get to answer the door.

"How's everything going?" she asked with a smile after she had visited with Amber for a few minutes and then sat down with us at the kitchen table.

"Great," I told her and Laci nodded.

"Good," Stacy said, nodding back. "She seems to be doing really well. I know her counselor is very pleased with her progress."

I glanced at Laci and smiled.

"Well," she said, the smile still on her face, "we're going to go ahead and schedule Amber's first unsupervised visit with Karen for this Saturday." (Karen was Amber's biological mother.) "These unsupervised visits will be longer than her supervised visits as we start moving toward reunification. I'll be picking her up at about nine o'clock in the morning and then returning her around four that afternoon. I'll talk to her before I leave today and let her know what's going to happen, and then you can-"

"Wait a minute," I interrupted. "What?"

"Well, if you'd rather be the one to tell her, that's fine, but-"

"No," I said, shaking my head. "I mean, what are you talking about? *Reunification?*"

"Well," Stacy explained. "Karen's met all of the requirements for us to begin permitting unsupervised visits. We'll start with unsupervised day visits and then work our way up to overnight and weekend-long visits. We'd like to try to get in about three full, unsupervised weekend visits before we permanently reunite them."

Permanently reunite them.

78

"I . . . I didn't know anything about this," I said. "How come we weren't told about this?"

"You knew that Karen had been paroled," Stacy pointed out. "I've taken her to visit her mother every month since she was released . . ."

"Well, yeah," I admitted. "But nobody ever said anything about her getting Amber back."

"As soon as Karen was released she filed a petition to regain full custody of Amber. The initial custody hearing was . . ." Stacy rifled through her papers looking for something, "umm, let's see . . . January twenty-fifth. That was right after she was assigned to me and I placed her with you. Anyway. There were several stipulations put in place at that hearing, and since then, Karen has met not only all of those requirements, but has also abided with all of the conditions of her parole. Now-"

"What kind of stipulations?"

"What do you mean?"

"You said there were stipulations put in place at the hearing. Like what?"

"Oh. Well, like she has to submit to random drug and alcohol testing. She's already enrolled in an outpatient treatment program and is attending weekly mental health sessions as part of that program. She's obtained full-time employment and has been attending substance abuse classes. She'll be required to undergo a final mental health assessment before she's released from the program and until then our department will make regular, unannounced home visits."

"*That's it?*"

"Those are standard measures," Stacy said, tipping her head at me. "We'll do everything we can to ensure that Karen is fit and able to provide the best care possible for Amber. We'll also maintain close contact for quite some time after Amber is returned to her mother."

I glanced at Laci. She looked at me sympathetically.

"But," I clarified, "if Karen drinks or takes drugs or drives drunk or anything like that-"

"Then Amber will remain a ward of the state," Stacy nodded. A look of relief must have crossed my face because she hastened to add, "But I don't think anything like that's going to happen. Karen's been working very hard and has made every effort to ensure that she'll regain custody of Amber. She's been clean since she went into prison over a year ago. I think it would be very reasonable to assume that she's going to fulfill all of the requirements and that her social worker will be encouraging the judge to grant custody. That's why we need to begin doing what we can now to help Amber get ready for the adjustment."

"When would it happen?" I asked, barely able to find my voice.

Stacy shuffled through her papers again. "Her final court date is the third Tuesday in August." She looked up at me and Laci. "I expect that Karen could very likely have physical custody of Amber within three months. Of course the state would retain legal custody for at least six months after that, but – if all goes well – Amber could be living with her mother permanently by the time school starts in the fall."

If all goes well?

Goes well for whom?

~ ~ ~

AFTER STACY LEFT, Laci and I looked at each other.

"She'll never make it," I said, shaking my head.

Laci looked at me questioningly.

"Karen," I explained. "She'll never make it. She'll get drunk or high and she'll fail her test or she'll get caught driving under the influence again or something. She'll never make it."

"Is that what you're hoping for?" Laci asked, obviously taken aback.

"Well, no," I said, hesitantly.

"Yes, you are!" Laci cried, aghast. "I can't believe this! You're *hoping* Karen will get put back in jail or something so that you can have her kid!"

"No, I'm not!" I argued. "But I just happen to think it's inevitable that she's gonna screw up and she's not going to be able to take care of Amber."

"I can't believe you," Laci said softly. "You need to be *praying* for this woman, not pulling for her to fail! You need to be praying for her that God will help her to stay clean and that she'll be able to be a wonderful mother to Amber."

"I am," I said weakly. Laci looked at me with a combination of disgust and disappointment on her face.

"I don't want her to fail," I insisted. "I . . . I just don't think that she's going to get Amber back."

"Why?" Laci asked. "Why would you think that?"

"I don't know," I said, giving her a small shrug. "That's just what I think."

"But you heard what Stacy just said."

"I know," I admitted, "but I'm pretty sure God's going to let Amber stay with us."

"Why?"

I paused.

"I think God told me that," I finally answered.

"What do you mean?"

"I dunno," I shrugged again. "I just think that God told me that."

"God *talked* to you about this?" Laci asked.

"Well," I hedged, "He didn't exactly *talk* to me, but . . ."

"But what?"

I didn't say anything for another minute. She kept staring at me.

"I don't know how to explain it," I confessed. "I've always kind of known that . . ."

I hesitated again.

"That what?"

"That she's always going to be ours," I said, reluctantly. "I don't know how to really explain it, but it's like I can see into the future or something and I just . . . I just somehow know that she's always going to be ours."

"You mean, like, you think we're going to adopt her?"

"I don't know," I shrugged.

She looked at me carefully.

"David," she finally said gently, "just because you've envisioned a future with Amber in it doesn't mean that that's what's going to happen."

"But why would God show me something like that if it wasn't true?"

"I don't think He did," she said, worriedly. "I don't think this idea you have is from *God.*"

"Why not?"

She opened her mouth, but then quickly closed it again and just looked at me.

"Why not?!" I asked again.

She didn't answer me.

"Because God told you that He wants us to move down to Mexico," I asked her angrily, "and you figure we can't do that as long as Amber's still with us?"

"I didn't say that!"

"You were thinking it!" I accused.

"I *do* want us to do God's will," Laci admitted, "but-"

"And you just assume that if God shows me something different than what He's told you, then obviously I'm the one who's wrong. I must be delusional."

"I never said that!" Laci cried.

"You think that you're the chosen one or something," I told her. "You think that you're the only one in this family that God could possibly talk to, don't you?"

"No," she said quietly. "I don't."

"Then why is it so hard for you to believe that maybe God showed me something?"

"Because I think that you love Amber very much," she said carefully, "and I think that you really don't want to lose her . . ."

I stared at her hard.

"And I think that it would be only natural for you to hope that she would become a part of our family and that you want her to stay with us."

"Don't you want her to stay with us?"

"I want what's best for her."

"You don't think we're best for her?"

"I think that if her mom wants her back and can take good care of her, then that's probably where she needs to be."

"And then we could go back to Mexico."

"This isn't about Mexico!" she cried. "This is about a mother being separated from her child! I can't believe you!"

"What about *me* being separated from her?" I asked, feeling tears sting the corners of my eyes for the first time. Laci looked at me sympathetically.

"You knew," she said gently. "You knew right from the start that she was probably going to go back to her mom one day."

"No," I answered, shaking my head and heading out of the room. "I didn't know."

Until then, I'd never worried that Amber might have to go back to live with her mother. Ever since she had come to live with us, I had felt in my heart that she would always be mine – and I had thought that God was the One who had put that certainty in my heart. I had been so sure that God wanted Amber to stay with me forever . . .

Until that day, it had never occurred to me that I might lose her.

I never saw it coming.

~ ~ ~

I FIGURED THAT Tanner was much more likely to see things my way (and I was sure that he wasn't going to urge me to pray for Amber's mother).

"I know it's just a matter of time before she does drugs again," I told him when I went over to his place to bemoan what Stacy had told me. "I just hope that she gets caught before she gets Amber back or before she goes out driving again and kills somebody."

"What makes you think she's gonna do drugs again?" Tanner asked. "She's been clean for a year."

"Yeah," I said, "but only because she was in *jail!* And right now they're giving her random drug tests all the time and everything, so if she drinks or does drugs then she's going right back in the slammer. But I guarantee you that as soon as her parole is over she's gonna go right back to her old ways."

"What makes you so sure?"

"Because that's what they all do," I said. "They get cleaned up for a while and then they start again and then they get cleaned up for a while and then they start back."

"They?" he asked, frowning at me.

"Druggies."

"You can't say that!" he snapped. "Just because somebody had a problem once with drugs doesn't mean that they can't get over it and change their lives."

I was taken aback by how indignant he suddenly seemed.

"I didn't mean-"

"You're a piece of work," he said, cutting me off. "You spend all day preaching at people that they need to clean up their acts and live right and everything, and then when someone actually tries to change, you say that they won't be able to do it."

85

I couldn't believe how furious he was, but then I suddenly remembered that his brother, Chase, had had some battles with drugs.

"I'm not saying people can't change," I said carefully. "I know people can change, but I just . . . I also know that it's not uncommon for someone to struggle with something like this for their whole life."

He didn't say anything. I went on cautiously.

"And I'm just saying that if Karen *is* going to have problems, I'd rather it happen now – before Amber goes back to live with her."

His face seemed to relax a little bit

"I don't want Amber to go back to her mom and get used to being with her and everything and then have to get put in foster care again. And what if her mom gets wasted or something and then drives with Amber in the car?"

"That's why she's got a social worker," Tanner said, "to make sure nothing like that happens."

"Yeah," I said, sardonically. "Because Social Services has done such a *great* job taking care of her so far."

"I think mostly you're just upset because you don't want to lose her."

"Well of *course* I don't want to lose her!"

He looked at me for a long moment.

"Sometimes you have to let go of people that you love," he said quietly. "It's not always about what *you* want, but about what's best for that person."

"*I'm* best for her."

"Look," he said quietly. "You might be, but if she's going to go back to her mom and you can't do anything about it . . ."

"What?"

"Then you have to let her go, and you need to do it in a way that's going to be best for her. This whole thing's gonna be hard enough on her. You can't get upset . . . you can't let her see you cry or anything like that – that'll just make things worse for her. You've gotta act like you're fine with it. Like it's what you want."

"I don't think I can do that," I said, my voice little more than a whisper.

"Yes, you can," he assured me. "You've just gotta keep telling yourself that you want her to be happy and that you're going to do everything you can to make this as easy on her as possible."

"I still think . . . I still think that maybe we're not going to lose her," I said. "I still think that maybe something's going to happen and she'll get to stay with me."

"Maybe," Tanner nodded, but he didn't look hopeful at all.

~ ~ ~

THINGS QUICKLY WENT from bad to worse. Sierra called during the first week of the summer to let me know that the sale of the cabin on Cross Lake had been finalized.

"I ran a search," she told me, "and there's a mobile home on the west shore that's got about one acre with it if you want to go see that."

"No thanks," I said miserably.

"I'll keep my eyes open and let you know when something else comes available," she offered.

"Yeah, thanks," I said. "That would be great."

Sierra never did call me again, but that was the least of my worries. Amber's unsupervised visits started the week before school got out and they increased in length and frequency all summer.

Each week we went to the pool as much as we could, letting Amber show off her new-found swimming skills to Dorito. Tanner took us every chance he had to Cross Lake so that we could pull the kids along behind his bass boat on an inner tube and let them catch bream and crappies from the deck of his pontoon. And every day I did everything I could think of to build wonderful memories with Amber and to enjoy every minute that I had with her.

But the reality that I was losing Amber – one unsupervised visit at a time – hung over every experience like a dark cloud. By the time August arrived, Amber was spending entire weekends with her mother and it was inevitable that she was going to be leaving us soon. All that stood between me and losing her forever was a final court hearing that was scheduled to take place a week and a half before school started.

I attended the hearing alone, hoping against hope that somebody was going to say *something* to the judge to let him know that Amber needed to stay with me. But Karen's social worker, Amber's counselor, her guardian ad litem and Stacy Reed all stated that they believed returning Amber to her mother was the best thing for everybody involved.

Nobody asked me what I thought.

After hearing what everybody had to say, the judge finally spoke.

"The court finds that the petitioner should regain physical custody of the child at this time. Legal custody will be retained by the state. Transfer should be completed within one week. After a period of six months, the petitioner may request that permanent, legal custody be restored and the court will consider such a request at that time. Is there anything else?"

Apparently not. The judge tapped his desk and adjourned for lunch.

Oh, God, I buried my face in my hands, covering my eyes. *Why are you doing this? WHY are you doing this? She has come so far with us and we've been so happy. There is no way that going back to live with that woman is going to be the best thing for Amber – for any of us.*

One week! How was I going to be able to let her go in one week?

"I know it's hard," I heard a soft voice say. I lifted my head from my hands and saw Stacy Reed looking down at me gently. I couldn't even nod or I was going to cry. She sat down next to me and put a hand on my shoulder. "Even though we know it's for the best, it's hard to say goodbye, isn't it? It'll be like this with every child you take in – some harder than others – but the pain is just something you're willing to endure because you know that you're helping these kids so much."

"Every child?" I asked.

"Most people – once they've fostered a child – decide they want to do it again. It's such a rewarding experience . . ."

I managed to shake my head at her. She looked at me sympathetically.

"You may feel differently after a while," she promised, "and we'd love to have you and Laci foster another child when you're ready."

I couldn't believe that I had just been told that Amber was going to be gone in less than a week and she was asking me to think about fostering another child.

"When will you take her?" I asked.

"I think she should have one more full-weekend visit beginning tomorrow, okay?" I managed a feeble nod. "Then she'll return to you late Sunday afternoon like usual and have a few days for closure at your house . . . to say goodbye. I'll pick her up Thursday morning – one week from today."

Say goodbye?

How was I ever going to be able to say goodbye to Amber?

~ ~ ~

WHEN STACY CAME to pick up Amber the next day, I asked her a question once Amber was buckled in the car and the doors were closed.

"I was wondering," I asked Stacy, "if we could still see Amber sometimes – after she's back with Karen?"

"It's usually a better idea to immerse the child in her new life and let her move forward."

"But is it – I mean, is it prohibited? Is it out of the question?"

"Well, no," Stacy hedged. "Ultimately it'll be up to Karen who Amber sees and who she doesn't see."

"So," I clarified, "if Karen agrees, then we can see her again, right?" Stacy nodded.

"Would you ask her?" I begged. "Would you just ask her if we can see Amber sometimes? It doesn't have to be anything big, just getting together at a restaurant to have a hamburger or meeting her in the park or something like that?"

"I'll ask her," Stacy agreed, opening her car door and sliding in. "But I don't think it's a good idea."

Amber was going to know that she was leaving us by the time she came back on Sunday afternoon. That meant that Dorito was going to need to know by then too. Laci and I sat down with him on the couch on Saturday and broke the news.

"When?" he asked in a small voice, looking up at Laci in dismay.

"Thursday," she said softly.

"Thursday!?" he cried.

She nodded at him and he jumped up from the couch and ran up the stairs into his bedroom. We heard his door slam and I leaned across the empty spot where he'd been and buried my face on Laci's shoulder. She reached her hand up to the back of my head and stroked my hair, resting her cheek on the top of my head. After a while I sat back up and wiped my eyes.

"I'll go talk to him," I whispered hoarsely, standing and trudging up the stairs toward his room.

I knocked on his door, but he didn't answer, so I tried the handle. It was locked.

"Dorito," I said, "let me in."

No answer.

I reached onto the top of the doorframe, grabbed the key we always kept there, and unlocked his door. He was lying on his bed – face down – with his head buried in his pillow.

"Dorito," I said quietly, sitting down on the edge of his bed. I rubbed my hand across his back. "Dorito, I'm sorry."

A sob racked his body. I leaned down and put my head on his, kissing his hair. "I'm sorry," I said again.

"I don't want her to leave!" he wept.

"I know you don't," I said. "I know."

"Can she still come over and play?" he asked, turning to look at me. His face was streaked with tears.

"I don't know," I admitted.

"Will she still go to school with me?" Dorito asked, wiping at his eyes.

I shook my head at him. "Her mom doesn't live in Cavendish," I said.

He somehow looked even more distressed.

"What if I ask God to let her stay here?" he asked after a moment, apparently struck with sudden inspiration. "Do you think He would let her stay if I pray?"

"I don't know, buddy," I said.

"God can do anything, right?" Dorito asked, sitting up excitedly and

92

obviously latching firmly onto this idea.

"Of course He can," I nodded.

"So He can make Amber stay with us if He wants to," Dorito confirmed.

I nodded again.

"So if I pray, then maybe she won't have to leave?"

"I don't know, Dorito," I said, shaking my head. "I don't want you to get your hopes up."

"But it might work," he said hopefully. "I'm gonna try. I'm gonna pray really, *really* hard. Okay?"

"I don't want you to get your hopes up," I warned him again, but he nodded happily. I looked at him and tousled his hair. Then I leaned forward and gave him a kiss on the forehead before I left.

I didn't have the heart to tell him that for weeks I'd been praying fervently for God to please let Amber stay with us . . . and evidently it hadn't been doing one bit of good.

Stacy brought Amber back late on Sunday afternoon and after Dorito had led Amber into the house, I rounded on her.

"Did you talk to Karen?" I asked. "Did you ask her if we can still see Amber sometimes?"

"She said, '*No*'," Stacy replied.

"You told her to say that," I accused quietly. "Didn't you?"

"It's not a good idea," she contended. "I know it's hard, but it's for the best. Trust me."

I gave her a look that I hoped conveyed just exactly how much I did not trust her.

"I'll pick her up at nine on Thursday morning," Stacy said, ignoring my look. "Enjoy your time with her until then. Okay?"

I finally nodded at her because I didn't have much choice, and then I went into the house.

The next three days flew by faster than seemed possible. I walked a fine line between acting happy for Amber that she was finally going to get to live with her mother where she truly belonged and letting her know how much I loved her and was going to miss her. I let her know that it was okay for her to be happy about living with her mom again – that we weren't mad at her – but I also let her know that it was okay if she was sad about leaving us and that if she wanted to, she could cry.

But she didn't. Not once. And neither did I.

Tanner would have been so proud.

Wednesday afternoon, Laci and I helped Amber pack her two new suitcases, filled with all the things she'd accumulated since she'd come to live with us.

"Your jacket's in the dryer," Laci told her. "I thought I'd wash it before you left. We'll put it in here before you zip it up, okay?" Laci patted one of the suitcases and Amber nodded at her.

"And I've got something for you," Laci told her. "I'll be right back."

She returned a moment later, holding a photo album which she handed to Amber. Amber took it from her and put it on her lap, opening it slowly.

Inside were most of the pictures that we'd taken in the past eight months since she'd first come to live with us. Pictures of her baking cookies with Laci and Lily in the kitchen. Pictures of her posing with Dorito and Lily in front of a snowman in our back yard and sledding in

94

our front. Helping me blow out the candles on my birthday cake. Holding a fish on Tanner's pontoon boat. Running in the three-legged race with Dorito at a church picnic. Blowing bubbles. Helping me wash the car. Splashing with Lily and Dorito in our hot tub. Standing at the Marin Headlands with the Golden Gate Bridge behind her. Posing with Tanner in front of a cable car. Dragging Lily down the aisle at Jordan and Charlotte's wedding. Dancing with me at their reception. Floating on her back at the pool.

"Thank you," she whispered softly to Laci when she'd finished looking through it.

"You're welcome, sweetie," Laci said, kissing her on the forehead. "I want you to always remember all the good times we had together – okay?"

Amber nodded.

"Okay," Laci said, squeezing her shoulder. "I'm going to go see if your jacket is dry."

After Laci had left the room I sat down next to Amber.

"I have a present for you, too," I said, handing her a little box.

She took it slowly from me.

"Open it," I urged. She took the lid off and pulled the necklace off of the cotton liner.

"You know what this is, right?" I asked her, pointing at the cross. She nodded. "So, I got you this because I want you to always remember everything that you've learned about Jesus, okay?"

She nodded again.

"I want you to remember that He died on the cross because He loved us all so much. I don't ever want you to forget that."

She ran a finger across the necklace.

"And," I went on, "I want you to remember me too. I don't ever want you to forget me and I want you to remember how much I love you."

I wrapped my arms around her and kissed the top of her head. I didn't tell her how much I was going to miss her because I knew I was going to start crying if I did.

"You want me to help you put it on?" I asked her. She nodded one more time and I put it around her neck.

"It looks pretty," I told her and she pressed it against her heart.

Laci returned with her jacket and stuffed it into Amber's suitcase. I already had her Bible packed in there and a letter addressed to Amber's mom. It was a letter begging her and begging her to *please* let us see Amber again . . . once she'd gone away from us.

~ ~ ~

TANNER CALLED LATE that afternoon.

"I wanted to ask if it would be alright if I came over to say goodbye to Amber?"

I nodded, unable to speak.

"Yeah," I finally managed to choke out. "Come on over."

Tanner always managed to show up at our house right around dinnertime and this night was no exception. When Laci asked him to join us, he pulled up his usual chair. It was good to have him there – somehow Tanner always managed to keep things fun even if everything was falling apart all around him.

"Third grade next week, huh?" he asked after we'd said grace, looking at Dorito and then at Amber. They both nodded at him.

"You know what happened to your daddy and me when we were in about the third grade?" he asked and their eyes lit up in anticipation of another one of Uncle Tanner's infamous stories.

"That is *not* an appropriate story," Laci informed him.

"The refrigerator one?"

"Yes."

"No," he said, shaking his head. "I wasn't going to tell that one."

"Good," Laci nodded, putting a roll on Lily's plate.

"What's the refrigerator one?" Dorito asked.

"Nothing," I said, hastily.

"Please?!" Dorito begged.

"No, my friends," Tanner said, "not tonight. Tonight I'm going to tell you a story about when Grandma and Grandpa Holland got a new hardwood floor in their living room!"

"Oh, brother," I muttered, and Tanner grinned at me.

"Yes," Tanner said in a dreamy voice. "I remember it as if it were yesterday. They'd left Jessica in charge . . ."

"Mistake number one," I pointed out, scooping a blob of potato casserole onto my plate.

"And they said I could come over and play while they were gone."

"Mistake number two."

Dorito grinned. "What happened?"

"Well," Tanner said after he'd taken a swallow of milk, "all the furniture was still moved out of the room and there was this nice, new, slippery hardwood floor to play on. So we took off our shoes and started sliding around on it in our socks. You know?"

Dorito and Amber both nodded.

"And then David decides to-"

"Oh!" I interrupted. "Don't *even* try to blame me for this. It was totally your idea!"

"My idea, perhaps," Tanner agreed, "but you're the one that went along with it."

"Like I had a choice."

"And," he said, "you're the one who went and got the furniture polish. I didn't even know where your mom kept it."

"Furniture polish?" Dorito asked.

"You know that stuff Mommy sprays on the tables and stuff that smells like lemons?"

He nodded.

"That's furniture polish," I told him.

"And if you read the back of it carefully," Tanner said, "it says: *Do not spray on floors.*"

"Ohhhhh," I moaned. "I got in so much trouble."

"Why?" Dorito asked.

"Because it made the floor slippery!" I cried.

"I thought you wanted it slippery," Dorito said.

"Not *that* slippery!"

"Why not?"

"Because every single person who walked into that room for the next three weeks fell down!" I said. "And the new area rug slid around on it for about a year!"

"Who fell down?"

"Everybody! Jessica. My mom. My dad. Everybody! My mom even cracked her elbow!"

"She let me sign her cast," Tanner said, cutting into his pork chop.

"Ohhhhh," I moaned again. "I got in *so* much trouble."

After dinner we settled into the living room. I knew that Tanner wouldn't stay long, wanting to give us time alone during our last evening together.

"I have something for you," he told Amber, motioning for her to come to him. She walked over to where he was and scrambled up onto the couch next to him, snuggling down beside him. Dorito hung on the edge of my chair, watching, while Laci sat in a chair with Lily on her lap. Tanner produced a ring and handed it to her. She held it with both hands, examining it carefully. It was a gold ring set with a round, white pearl.

"Do you know what this is?" he asked her, pointing to the pearl. She nodded and whispered in his ear.

"Right," he agreed. "Do you know who makes pearls?"

She whispered in his ear again.

"Good," he smiled, patting her on the back. "You're a smart little girl."

She smiled at him.

"Do you know *why* oysters make pearls?"

She shook her head.

"Well," he said, "sometimes a little piece of sand or something gets inside of an oyster and it starts bothering him, but he can't spit it out . . . you know? It gets stuck."

She nodded.

"So what the oyster does, is he starts coating it with this smooth white stuff." Tanner ran his large finger over the surface of the pearl. "He just keeps adding layers and covering up the grain of sand and making it all smooth so it doesn't bother him anymore."

Amber stared at the ring more intently and Dorito wandered closer, peering at it.

"So," Tanner said, tapping the pearl, "down inside here is a piece of sand that used to bother the oyster, but he just kept working and working at it until he turned it into something beautiful."

Laci and I glanced at each other, but then I quickly looked away.

"Everybody has stuff that bothers them," Tanner went on. "I'm giving you this because I want you to remember what the oyster does – he just keeps on working and working until he turns his problems into something beautiful that don't bother him anymore. Can you remember that?"

Amber turned her face to Tanner, smiled at him and nodded.

"Let's see a finger," he said and she held a hand up to him.

"I'm afraid it's kind of big," he worried. It was woefully large, even when he slid it onto her thumb. "I just wanted to make sure you could wear it even when you were older."

He looked at me unhappily. "I should have got a different size."

"Show Tanner your necklace," I told Amber. She pulled her necklace out from her shirt.

"That's beautiful," Tanner said. "Where'd you get it?"

Amber pointed at me.

"Maybe you could keep your ring on there until it fits one of your fingers," I suggested. "Would you like to do that?"

She nodded and Tanner helped her undo the clasp and slip the ring onto the chain with the cross.

A few minutes later, Tanner hugged Amber goodbye and headed for the door. I tried to follow him — to walk out with him and thank him for coming by — but he went way too fast. I watched after him from the front door and saw him wiping his eyes as he headed for his truck.

You can't get upset . . . you can't cry.

Isn't that what he'd told me?

What a hypocrite.

~ ~ ~

UNLIKE DORITO (WHO had been known to lay awake for hours, talking to himself), Amber usually fell right to sleep shortly after we put her in bed. But tonight – when I checked on her twenty minutes later – she was wide awake.

"You okay?" I asked her and she nodded.

The next time I went back in – another twenty minutes later – she was *still* awake.

"Having a hard time getting to sleep?" I asked her.

She nodded.

I sat down on the edge of her bed and picked up her hand.

"It's going to be okay," I told her. "You and your mom are going to be really happy together."

She pulled my head down close to hers.

"I'm going to miss you," she whispered in my ear.

"I know," I whispered back. "I'm going to miss you too."

More than you'll ever know.

It was dark, so I figured she would never know if there were a few tears in my eyes.

"What if I need someone to take care of me again?" she wanted to know.

"You mean . . . you mean if your mom has to . . . go away again?"

She nodded in the darkness.

"If you ever need me," I promised her, "I'll be right here. I'll always be here for you."

I could barely make out her eyes shimmering in the dark.

"Okay?" I asked, and she nodded.

"Try to go to sleep now," I said, kissing her on the forehead and putting her hand back down on the mattress. "You've got a big day ahead of you tomorrow."

102

She nodded and I left.

When I returned thirty minutes later, she was at last asleep. It was then that I finally let myself drop down on my knees next to her bed and cry over her. I begged God some more to *please* not take her from me, although I had long ago given up any hope that He might let her stay.

I'd been in there for quite a while when Laci came in.

"Come to bed," she urged, gently laying her hand on my shoulder.

"No," I said, shaking my head. She knelt down on the floor next to me and put an arm around me.

"You can't stay in here all night," she said softly.

"Why not?" I asked.

She looked at me for a long time and then finally stroked my hair and kissed me tenderly on the forehead. She got up and left without saying another word. I sat on the floor with my head on Amber's bed and I held her hand as she slept, her breathing slow and soft and steady. I fell asleep off and on throughout the night, but for the most part I was awake, praying for her and begging God to change His mind, and crying because I knew I was losing her. In the morning I left her room when the sun started peeking in through the window.

Strangely, all of my crying the night before must have gotten it out of my system because I didn't cry one single tear when Stacy loaded Amber into the car for the last time and I said goodbye to her.

I turned to Laci after we'd waved while the car disappeared from sight. There were tears glistening in her eyes and she reached her hand out to my arm in a comforting manner.

"I didn't sleep very good last night," I told her. She looked surprised that these were the first words out of my mouth, but then she nodded. "I'm going to go lay down for a little bit. I'm exhausted."

"Okay," she said.

Dorito was dabbing at his eyes, but I barely paid any attention to him as I went past him and into the house. I kicked off my shoes and laid down on the bed with my clothes still on, pulling the blankets up around me to ward off the chill that seemed to be hanging in the air. Then I fell into a deep and dreamless sleep.

The next thing I knew, Laci was shaking me gently awake.

"David?" she said softly.

"What?" I asked, sitting up suddenly.

"Lily wants to go to the pool," she said. "It looks like it might be rainy the next few days, so it might be our last chance before school starts. I thought I'd take them."

"Okay," I nodded.

"Do you want to go?" she asked.

"What time is it?" I asked groggily, looking my watch.

"It's after one," she said.

I had been asleep for over three hours already, but I don't remember when I'd ever felt so fatigued.

"I don't think I'm up for it," I said. She nodded understandingly and I said, "You go ahead and go, though."

"Okay," she agreed. "Do you want me to make you some lunch before we leave?"

"No," I said. "I'll get myself something in a little bit."

"Okay. We'll be back in time for dinner."

I nodded and put my head back down, too tired to even think about eating.

I fell asleep again and didn't wake up until I heard the garage door opening. I looked at my watch and was surprised to find that it was now after five o'clock. I was still exhausted and – even though I'd had nothing to eat all day – wasn't the least bit hungry. I managed to make myself put on my shoes, however, and went into my office. I was sitting in front of the computer screen, staring unfocused at the image before my eyes, by the time Laci unloaded the kids.

"How are you doing?" she asked kindly, standing in the doorway of my office.

"Fine," I said, not looking away from the computer screen.

"What did you have for lunch?"

"A sandwich," I told her. Then I remembered that we'd used up the last of the bread that morning because Dorito and Amber had both wanted toast. I turned and looked at her. "I wasn't hungry."

She nodded and walked over to me.

She bent down and kissed my cheek and I wrapped my arm around her waist, giving it an absent-minded squeeze.

"Did you guys have fun at the pool?" I asked her.

"Yeah," she said, and I figured she was lying to me, too. "I'm going to go start dinner now."

"Okay," I said. "Let me know if you need any help."

That was Thursday – a normal workday for me. Because I had spent most of the day in bed, by the time dinner was over (which I'd eaten even though I had no appetite and it tasted like cardboard) I found that I had about eight hours of work still lying in front of me. I settled down in front of the computer at about seven o'clock and tried to concentrate.

At eight, Laci informed me that Lily was ready for bed. I saved what little work I'd been able to do, went into her bedroom to kiss her goodnight, and then returned to my computer.

At nine, Laci let me know that Dorito was now ready to go to sleep.

"Can you send him in here?" I asked. "I'm really behind."

"Sure," she nodded, and before long, Dorito padded in for his goodnight kiss.

At eleven o'clock, Laci stuck her head in the door one more time.

"Gonna be ready for bed pretty soon?" she asked.

I rubbed my eyes. "I don't know," I said. "I've actually got a lot to do."

"Do you want me to wait up for you?"

"No," I said. "I don't know how long I'll be. You go ahead without me."

She agreed, kissed me goodnight, and went to bed.

It was after four in the morning by the time I finally crawled into bed next to her. Even though I had put in more than my usual eight hours, I still hadn't accomplished what I'd needed to, but I couldn't keep my eyes open any longer and I fell asleep almost as soon as my head hit the pillow.

In the morning, when the alarm sounded, I turned it off and rolled back over.

"You came to bed late last night," Laci observed.

"Yeah," I agreed.

"You going to get up?" she asked.

"Not yet," I said. "I'm gonna try to get a bit more sleep."

She paused for a moment, but finally said, "Okay," and got out of bed without me.

It was noon by the time I pulled myself out of bed and dragged myself into my office. Just like the night before, everything seemed to take me longer than it usually did. I had to work until midnight just to get the bare minimum done.

I only slept until ten the next morning. Usually I didn't work on Saturdays, but I was so far behind that I spent most of the day in my office, trying to catch up.

Sunday we went to church and then out to eat at a restaurant afterward. I ordered something, couldn't eat most of it, went home, and went back to bed.

Monday was Dorito's first day of school. I got up in time to take him to school, but passed on breakfast when Laci offered it to me and then I locked myself in my office. At lunch time, Laci asked me if I wanted something to eat and I told her, "No." About fifteen minutes later, however, she showed up with a plate of macaroni and cheese and a hot dog.

"I said I didn't want anything," I told her.

"You have to eat," she insisted.

The macaroni and cheese was mushy, with absolutely no taste at all. The hot dog was rubbery and the bun stale. Laci made the mistake of leaving after I'd eaten two bites of the hot dog and one forkful of the macaroni and cheese. I fed the rest to the dog and let Laci feel satisfied when she returned in a little while to pick up an empty plate.

When Dorito came home from school he trooped into my office and proudly announced that he had math homework.

"Will you help me?" he asked.

"Tonight?"

"Yeah. It's due tomorrow."

"I don't know if I can tonight," I said, shaking my head. I indicated my computer and my desk. "I've got a lot to do."

"But you've been working all the time!" Dorito complained.

"I'm sorry," I said. "I've gotta get this stuff done. I'm sure Mom can help you."

"Mom?"

"Yeah."

"But you said the only time I was ever supposed to ask her for help with math was when you're not home!"

"And when I'm really busy," I said. "I'll try to help you next time."

But the next time Dorito needed help with math I was also too busy. (Or maybe I was too tired – it was hard to keep track.) It seemed that all I did was sleep, eat enough tasteless food to keep Laci off my back, or work. And even though I was working more hours than I ever had before, I seemed to be getting less and less done. It felt as if I were trudging through quicksand.

Two weeks after Dorito had started school, Laci had had enough. She came into my office, sat down on the couch, and told me that she wanted to talk.

"What?" I asked, not turning away from my computer.

"Look at me," she said.

"What do you want?" I asked, glancing at her. "I've got a lot to do."

"You've always got a lot to do," she said. "Come here and talk to me." She patted the couch next to her. I sighed heavily, stood up, and walked reluctantly over to the couch. I sat down.

"What?" I said again.

"I'm worried about you," she said gently.

"Worried about me?" I asked. "Why?"

"You're not eating right," she began, "you're tired all the time. If you're not in bed you're in here in front of the computer-"

"I'm working," I reminded her.

"No," she said, shaking her head. "You're burying yourself in your work and you're shutting everybody out."

"No, I'm not," I argued. "I've got a lot to do."

"David," she said, tipping her head at me.

"What?"

She sighed and looked away.

"I know you miss Amber," she said quietly, looking back at me, "but you can't just keep closing everybody out the way you've been doing."

"I haven't been," I insisted. "I've just been really busy-"

"And really tired?"

"Well, yeah," I admitted. "Because I've been working so hard."

She looked at me for a long moment.

"You hardly spend three minutes a day with the kids," she complained. "Dorito's been working on a family tree project for social studies and you haven't even looked at it. You've missed his last two soccer games and Lily has to come find you if she wants a kiss goodnight – you don't even tuck her in anymore!"

"Things will get better once I'm caught up," I promised.

"I think you need to go see someone," she finally said.

"See someone?"

108

"Yeah," she nodded. "Like a doctor or something."

"I don't need a doctor."

"Or just somebody you can talk to . . . somebody that can help you."

"I don't need any help," I insisted, patting her on the leg. "I just need to get caught up and then I'll be fine."

She opened her mouth to argue, but I interrupted.

"And me sitting here – talking with you – isn't helping."

She looked at me doubtfully.

"I'm fine," I said, leaning forward and kissing her on the cheek. "I appreciate you worrying about me, but I'm fine. Now why don't you go and make some lunch and then I'll come down and eat with you and Lily after a little bit."

"Okay," she finally nodded, reluctantly, and then she went away to make another cardboard lunch that I had to force myself to join them for and choke down.

Another week passed and I still was behind at work. Food was still bland and flavorless. I still fell instantly asleep the moment my head hit the pillow.

After dinner one night I was in front of my computer, like usual, when Laci knocked on my office door.

"Can I interrupt?" she asked.

"Sure," I said, turning toward her.

"I just talked to Danica."

"What'd she want?"

"She and Mike were thinking about coming to visit this weekend."

"Really?" I asked, surprised. Mike and Danica were two of the busiest people I knew . . . they hardly ever came to visit.

"They both had the weekend free and they haven't been here in a long time," she shrugged. "It's okay, isn't it?"

"Sure. That'd be great."

She smiled at me. "Great," she said, turning to leave. "I'll tell them to come on."

Mike and I had grown up together and he had always been one of my best friends. He and his wife, Danica, lived in Minnesota. The fact that Mike was a general physician and Danica was a psychiatrist should have tipped me off that something was up, but it didn't.

~ ~ ~

WE MADE ARRANGEMENTS for Dorito and Lily to have a sleepover at my sister's house Friday night. By the time Mike and Danica arrived on Friday evening, the kids were already gone, looking forward to spending the night and following day with their cousins.

It was good to have Mike and Danica there. I barely noticed how bland the dinner tasted as we smiled and laughed and swapped stories. Sometimes I found that I wasn't really paying attention to what was being said and someone would have to repeat something for me, but overall I did pretty good. It was the closest I had felt to normal in three weeks.

After dinner, Mike and I went out onto the back deck while Laci and Danica remained behind in the kitchen to clean up and get dessert ready.

"What's Dorito in now?" Mike asked. "Third grade?"

"Uh-huh."

"Is he having a good school year so far?"

"Yeah, I think so."

Mike nodded and looked out into the yard for a minute.

"The trees are supposed to be really pretty this fall," he mused. "They say when you have a warm, wet spring like we did, the colors are supposed to be better."

"Oh," I nodded.

"Of course if we get an early frost, that could turn 'em brown and make 'em fall early."

"Oh."

I really hated small talk. Mike apparently appreciated it about as much as I did because he finally quit trying to make it. The next thing out of his mouth wasn't small talk.

"I was really sorry to hear that you lost Amber," Mike said quietly after a moment.

I didn't answer, wishing he hadn't mentioned her. The knot that

111

always seemed to be lingering in my stomach suddenly tightened.

"You ever hear how she's doing?"

"No."

"That's gotta be hard," he said. I nodded.

"You wanna talk about it?"

I shook my head.

"Sometimes," he said, "when something like this happens, it's good to talk about it with somebody. Somebody who's not really involved in the situation."

That's when I suddenly realized that Mike and Danica had not just randomly decided to pay us a visit and I understood why Tanner hadn't been invited to join us for dinner as he normally would have been.

"Laci called you!" I accused.

He didn't answer me.

"She shouldn't have done that," I said angrily.

"She's worried about you-"

"She shouldn't have made you drive all the way here to see me for nothing!"

"It's not for nothing-" he began, but I cut him off again.

"And I don't appreciate her going behind my back!" I said, slamming my hand down on the deck rail. "I can't *believe* that she did this!"

"When you lost Gabby," Mike said, "and Laci went through a hard time, *you* called me."

Gabby was our first child. She had been stillborn and Laci had gone through a period of depression after we'd lost her.

"That was different."

"How?" he asked. "How is it any different?"

"Because Laci needed medicine," I said, "and I don't."

"How do you know?"

"I don't need drugs!" I cried. "Drugs aren't going to help!"

"What will help?"

112

"If I had Amber back," I said crossly, "that would help! Or if I could at least find out if she's okay somehow . . . that would help!"

"You need to put Amber in God's hands," Mike said gently. He loves her even more than you do . . ."

"That doesn't mean nothing bad's going to happen to her!"

"No," he admitted, "I know."

"So you'll forgive me if I don't think drugs are the ticket here?"

"Maybe it would help if you talked to someone," he suggested again.

"Maybe it would help if you stayed out of it," I snapped back.

He let out his breath and turned away.

"You know," he said after a minute, turning back to me, "when I was little and my dad was so sick, he could hardly ever play with me."

I looked away from him and didn't say anything.

"But," he went on, "I always knew it wasn't his fault. I knew he couldn't help it . . ."

He paused for a minute. I still didn't say anything.

"Is Dorito going to be able to say that one day?" Mike asked bluntly. "Is he going to say, 'My dad couldn't help it,'? Or is he going to spend his whole life wondering why you didn't do everything you could to be the same kind of a father to him that you were before Amber went away?"

"This is none of your business," I said sharply and I stalked into the house.

"You can quit giving us time to talk," I snapped at Laci. "We're done," and I stormed out the front door and walked to the end of the block. I turned around and came back, finally sitting on our front stoop and staring into the starry night sky for a long time.

Mike was right – I knew that. I knew that I had to do *something* to pull myself together. I thought about Dorito and Lily and how they needed me, just like Mike had said.

I kept expecting Mike or Laci to come out and try to talk to me, but neither one did, so finally I went back through the house and onto the deck, finding them all quietly eating cheesecake.

"You want some dessert?" Laci asked me gently when I stepped through the sliding glass door.

"Who made it?"

"Have you ever seen me making cheesecake?" she wanted to know with a small smile.

"Well, if Danica made it, I guess I'll have some . . ."

"Yeah," Mike laughed. "As if Danica could ever make cheesecake."

Danica swatted him and we all laughed and I sat down to eat store bought cheesecake among people who loved me enough to forgive me no matter how I treated them.

The next day Tanner took us all out on his pontoon boat and that evening, when Jessica brought Dorito and Lily back, all of us were in the hot tub.

For the entire day, no one mentioned Amber . . .

Or therapy . . .

Or drugs . . .

It was a good day.

Sunday we went to the early church service and then to a restaurant for brunch. Ever since the cheesecake Friday night, food had actually started to have some taste again. I still wasn't terribly hungry, but I managed to go through the buffet line twice.

"Have you thought about what I said?" Mike ventured tentatively when we got home.

"Yeah," I said. "I know you were right. I'll do better – I promise."

"You might need some help," he worried. "It's not always easy to do on your own."

"I'm not taking any drugs."

"I didn't say you needed drugs," he said. "But you might. Or you

114

might need counseling-"

"No," I said, shaking my head determinedly. "I don't wanna see a shrink."

"They're not all bad, you know," he said, glancing out onto the deck where his wife and Laci were drinking coffee and watching the kids play in the back yard.

"Sorry," I mumbled. "No offense."

"Why don't you talk to her for a few minutes?" Mike suggested.

"No," I said adamantly, shaking my head.

"Why not?"

"No."

"What are you so afraid of ?" he asked.

"I don't know," I admitted.

"You don't even have to lay down on a couch or anything," he smiled. "You two could just go for a walk or something."

I didn't answer him.

"She's *right here*," he persisted quietly.

I looked away and thought for a minute. They had made a special trip just to try and help me. And Dorito and Lily needed me to get better. I finally looked back at Mike and gave him a tight nod. Then I went out onto the front porch, sat down, and waited until he sent Danica out to find me.

When she joined me I didn't look at her – I just kept staring straight ahead. She didn't say anything, but she sat down next to me on the top step.

"I don't want to do this," I finally told her, still not looking in her direction.

"Do what?"

"Tell you what's bothering me. Have a big psychological breakthrough. Get in touch with my inner feelings."

I glanced at her and saw that she was smiling.

"What do you want?" she asked kindly.

"I just want to get better."

"How will you know when you're better?"

"I'll be a good dad and a good husband."

"You don't think you're a good dad and a good husband?"

"No," I said, shaking my head. "Not right now. I can't do anything right now. I feel . . . I kinda feel like I'm underwater."

She nodded.

"Can you fix me?" I asked, glancing at her again.

She laughed outright. "You know my specialty is eating disorders, right?"

I smiled back at her.

"Okay," she said, bringing her hands together. "Let me get this straight. You want me to 'fix' you, but you don't want to take drugs, have a psychological breakthrough, or get in touch with your inner feelings. That sound about right?"

I nodded at her.

"Okay," she agreed with another kind smile on her face. "Here's a couple of things that I think you should do."

116

~ ~ ~

THE FIRST THING Danica wanted me to do was to force myself to get out of the house and go do something fun – whether I felt like having fun or not. I had to admit that I had felt better on Saturday when we'd all spent the day on the lake than I had at any other point since Amber had left. So that evening, after Mike and Danica had gone, I called Tanner. Then I went into my office where Dorito was sitting in front of the computer, playing a game.

He turned to look at me when I came in.

"Hi."

"Hi."

I sat down on the couch.

"I just talked to Tanner," I said.

"About what?"

"About fishing. He says he can take us next Saturday – we can get up early in the morning and go all day. Just the three of us."

"No," he said, shaking his head. "I don't wanna go."

"What?"

"I don't want to," he said again, returning to his game.

"Why not?"

"I dunno," he shrugged, clicking away at his keyboard.

"Dorito," I said, sternly. He turned reluctantly to look at me. "Why don't you want to go?"

"I don't know," he said again. "I just don't want to."

I looked at him for a minute. He stared back at me resolutely.

"Okay," I finally said. "If you change your mind, let me know."

He nodded and went back to his game and I walked out into the hall. I stopped at the top of the stairs, wondering about what had just happened. Never before in his life had Dorito turned down a chance to go fishing – ever. I stood there for a moment, thinking, and after I'd thought for a minute I turned around and went back into the office.

"Hi," I said again.

"Hi."

"Got a minute?"

He gave me something between a nod and a shrug and turned to face me. I sat down on the couch again and patted the spot next to me. "Come sit here," I said.

He got up and came over, sitting down next to me.

I put my arm around him and gave him a squeeze.

"I love you," I said.

"I love you, too."

"Dorito?"

He looked up at me, expectantly. I looked back into his black eyes.

"You miss Amber," I said, gently. "Don't you?"

He nodded slightly.

"I do, too," I said, nodding. "I haven't felt like doing much of anything since she left."

He didn't answer me.

"But," I went on, "we've got each other and we still have our lives to live. We have to keep going."

He still didn't say anything.

"I know it's hard," I said.

He just looked at me.

"But we have to go on. Do you understand what I'm saying?"

He nodded.

"So, will you go fishing with me?"

He shook his head slowly.

"Why not, Dorito?"

Tears welled up in his eyes and he looked down into his lap and shook his head some more.

"Dorito," I said, wrapping my arm around him again. I tipped his chin up toward me so that he was looking at me again. "Dorito, we need

118

to do this. We need to get out of here and go fishing together. Or we can go to the gun range and get some target practice in or we can go to the park and ride our bikes or-"

He started crying hard, bringing his hands up to cover his face.

I stopped talking to him and just held him for a bit and let him cry. I kissed his hair and rested my cheek on the top of his head while he sobbed.

"I'm sorry," he finally choked.

"You don't have to be sorry," I told him. "It's okay to cry." (Crying was actually the other thing that Danica had wanted me to work on.)

"No," he said. "It's my fault."

"What?" I asked, not sure I'd heard him correctly.

"It's my fault."

"What's your fault?"

"That Amber's gone."

"*What?* That's ridiculous! It's not your fault."

"Yes, it is," he wept.

"Dorito," I said, shaking him gently. "How is it your fault that Amber's gone?"

"I was mad at her," he cried. "I wanted her to go away."

I felt my breath catch in my throat.

"Dorito," I said quietly. "That's not why she's gone."

"Yes it is," he insisted. "I told God I didn't want her to be my sister anymore."

I tipped his chin so that he was facing me.

"I didn't mean it," he whispered desperately.

"I know you didn't," I said. "Just because you prayed something like that doesn't mean that's why Amber's gone. That's not how it works."

"How does it work?" he asked in a small voice, looking at me, pleadingly.

I have no idea.

I shook my head at him.

"God has a plan for us," I said. "For you, for me, for Amber. He would never take Amber away just because you prayed something like that. He's not going to take her away unless that's what was going to be best."

"Best for who?"

"Best for all of us."

"How is it best for us?" he wanted to know.

"I . . . I don't know," I admitted. "But one day we will know. One day we'll see that God had everything under control – even when we couldn't figure out what He was doing."

I could tell that he wasn't too convinced, but it was the best I could do.

"But, Dorito," I went on, "I know one thing for sure. I know that it is not your fault that Amber is gone. I know you feel bad about what you did, but you have to know that it's not your fault. It's not."

He buried his face into my chest and let me hold him for another minute. Finally he sat up and wiped his eyes.

"I really do want to go fishing with you," I said, cupping his chin toward me again. "Will you come?"

He nodded.

"Good," I smiled. "Somebody's gotta help me keep Tanner in line."

So. Thing number two. Crying.

Danica had said that I needed to grieve over losing Amber. She said that it wasn't good that I hadn't cried since Amber had left.

When Laci had made the photo album for Amber, she had made one for us at the same time, so now I pored over it every day – remembering Amber and missing her. I grieved for her like Danica had told me to and it hurt. It hurt *a lot*. But bit by bit, things actually started to get better and I found that each day it hurt a little less. Forcing myself to get out and do

120

fun stuff seemed to help too. The fishing trip with Tanner appeared to send Dorito on his way to getting better as well, and by the time the leaves started changing at the beginning of October, things seemed almost normal.

~ ~ ~

THE SECOND FRIDAY in October had been an optional teacher workday and Tanner had picked Dorito up early in the morning to "help" him coach the high school football team's three-hour practice. Tanner had planned to take Dorito out to lunch afterward and then swing by the house to pick me up so that we could all go to the gun range to site in our rifles for deer season in the afternoon.

Lily – who had the capacity to keep herself entertained like no child I'd ever seen before – was in her bedroom, playing with her stuffed animals. Earlier, when I had walked by her room, I'd noticed that she had about twenty of them spread across the floor of her room, each with a little piece of fake, plastic food sitting in front of them. In an effort to force myself to have fun, I had stepped into Lily's room and joined them all for a mid-morning snack.

Just before lunch I was in my office, researching some materials for a project in Massachusetts, when the doorbell rang. I didn't pay much attention to it, but I guess in the back of my mind I figured it was Tanner (even though that made absolutely no sense at all because Tanner never bothered to knock or ring the bell and it was way too early for him to be bringing Dorito home anyway). I didn't think about this though. I ignored the bell and let Laci get the door.

Soon I heard voices – Laci talking to someone. It wasn't until the conversation had been going on for quite a while that it registered with me that the dialogue was in Spanish, that Laci wasn't talking to Tanner, and that I had absolutely no idea who was in our house.

I got up and went down the stairs and into the living room. There was a heavy-set Hispanic woman, probably in her mid- forties, seated on

122

the couch next to Laci. They both looked up when I came into the room. Laci spoke first.

"*Me gustaría que conozcas a mi esposo,*" Laci said, her voice strangely unsteady. *I'd like for you to meet my husband.* "*Este es* David."

The woman stood up.

"David," Laci said, gesturing to the woman. "*Esta es Savanna Escalante.*"

"*Hola,*" I said, extending my hand toward her. She tentatively shook it. I sat down in a chair and Savanna Escalante and Laci returned to the couch. I looked at Laci.

You know how thoughts can run through your mind very quickly? How – in just a second – your mind can manage to develop an entire scenario to explain something that doesn't make sense to you?

There's a strange woman in my living room speaking Spanish. We have lived here for over three years. Dorito was starting to lose some of his Spanish. We still tried to speak it frequently and keep him fluent, but it wasn't the same as having him immersed in it like he'd been when we lived in Mexico.

In a flash, that's what I figured this must be about – that Laci had hired someone to help Dorito keep up with his Spanish. I sat on the couch and smiled at her and wondered how much she charged and if we really needed to hire someone and why hadn't Laci talked to me about this first?

And then Laci spoke.

"David," she said, looking at me. "Mrs. Escalante came here to see us from Mexico City."

Laci's eyes searched my face, trying to make sure that she had my attention.

"She came here to meet Dorito," she said slowly.

"Uh-huh," I nodded and looked back at the woman. I was still smiling. I wondered if we shouldn't consider hiring someone who was already a US citizen so that we didn't have to worry about employment regulations and everything. I wondered why Laci hadn't made arrangements for her to meet Dorito when Dorito was actually *here* . . .

"David," Laci said. She was still searching my face and when I looked back at her, her eyes locked into mine.

"What?" I felt my smile disappear.

"Mrs. Escalante . . ." Laci seemed unable to go on. She looked as if she were on the verge of tears.

"What?" I asked again. "What's going on?"

"She's here," Laci said, swallowing hard, "because . . ."

"Because what?" I asked when she stopped once more.

Laci took a moment, apparently resolving to finish her sentence the next time she spoke.

"She's here," Laci finally said, looking at me nervously, "because she's Dorito's biological mother."

~ ~ ~

"WHAT?"

"MRS. ESCALANTE is Dorito's mother."

"No," I said, shaking my head back and forth.

"Yes," Laci said.

"*Dorito no es su hijo,*" I told her.

Dorito is not your son.

"*Sí,*" she said, nodding emphatically. "*Sí, hablé con el orfanato. Mi niño está aquí con usted.*"

Yes. Yes, I spoke with the orphanage. My little boy is here with you.

"*Tú no sabes eso,*" I said to Mrs. Escalante. *You don't know that.*

"*Sí. Sí lo sé. Mi hijo está aquí contigo.*"

Yes. Yes, I do. My son is here with you. She was nodding her head vigorously. "*Me gustaría verlo.*"

I would like to see him.

"Absolutely not!" I said. "*¡Absolutamente no!*"

"David!" Laci cried.

"She's not seeing him," I snapped.

"*Él estaba en el parque-*"

He was in the park-

"*¡Tú no sabes nada de él!*" I insisted. *You don't know anything about him.*

"*Mi esposo lo llevó al parque,*" she tried to tell me.

My husband took him to the park.

I pointed at the door. "Get out! *¡Fuera!*"

"*Sólo quiero verlo.*"

I just want to see him.

"I want you to leave now!" I shouted over Laci's protests. She either spoke a bit of English or she figured out my body language pretty quick, because she stood up and followed me to the door.

"*No quiero causar problemas . . .*"

I don't want to cause any problems . . .

"Please," Laci was saying. "David, please listen to her!"

"No, Laci!" I yelled at her. "Shut-up!"

I opened the door and indicated to Savanna Escalante that she should leave. She was talking a blue streak now, I could barely catch any of what she was saying. When she got outside and turned around to face me, there were tears streaming down her cheeks. I slammed the door in her face and wheeled on Laci. She had tears on her cheeks too.

"You don't even know what she wanted!" Laci cried.

"She wants to take my son away from me!"

"You don't know that! The least you could have done was-"

But I wasn't listening. I was already halfway down the hall and into the bathroom, slamming the door on her too.

I rushed to the toilet, leaned over it, and threw up.

126

~ ~ ~

AFTER I THREW up, I sank down against the wall and drew my knees up to my body, resting my head on them and sobbing quietly.

You cannot *take Dorito too,* I begged God. *I will not survive if You take him away from me. Please don't take Dorito away too. PLEASE DO NOT take Dorito away from me.*

I don't know how long I sat there like that, pleading with God to not let me lose Dorito, but when I finally finished I had resolved that I was going to do whatever was within my power to keep that woman from taking Dorito from me. I stood and washed my face and then I pulled my phone out and called Tanner.

"Hi, Daddy!"

"Dorito . . ." I said, my lungs barely able to draw in any air.

"Tanner let me answer his phone," he said.

"I see that."

"'Cause he knew it was you."

"I love you," I told him, my voice catching. I felt fresh tears stinging my eyes.

"I love you, too," he said, matter-of-factly. "Do I have to go home now?"

"Pretty soon," I said.

"Awwww," he said. "We just got here!"

"Where?"

"*Wilma's,*" he said. "I'm getting a *footlong* hotdog."

"A footlong," I said. "Wow! Can I talk to Tanner?"

"Okay."

After a moment Tanner came on the line.

"Yo, what's up?"

"Don't let Dorito out of your sight, okay?"

"What?"

"I'll be there in a few minutes. Wait for me. Don't leave him alone for one second."

"What's wrong?"

"Nothing," I said. "Everything. I don't know. Just . . . just wait there for me and don't take your eye off of him. Okay?"

"Okay," Tanner said, and then, "do you want me to bring him home?"

I closed my eyes.

"No," I said after a moment. "I'll come there. Just . . . just enjoy your hotdogs and I'll see you in a little bit. But don't leave him."

"I won't."

I hung up the phone and opened the door to the bathroom. I found Laci sitting on the floor in the hallway. She looked up at me with a tear-streaked face.

"You can't keep him from her," she said quietly. "It's not right."

"Not right?!" I exclaimed. "You wanna know what's *not right*, Laci?"

She looked at me.

"What's not right is that anybody who wants to can just have a baby and then decide that maybe they'll take care of it or maybe they won't! Maybe they'll just leave it in the park because they didn't feed him right and so he got rickets and now he can't walk and they're like, 'Oh! I don't wanna take care of him anymore!'"

I saw new tears come in to Laci's eyes. I kept going.

"It's not right that somebody can have a little girl and then decide that they'd rather do drugs or something instead of taking care of her and so then she has to go into a foster home and get molested by some perverted teenager!"

The tears rolled down Laci's cheeks.

"But do you want to know what's REALLY not right, Laci?" I yelled. She started crying harder. "What's really not right is that people like you and me try to help these kids and we fall in love with them and then these lousy excuses for parents can come in and just take them back any time

128

they want and you and I are left holding the pieces. *That's what's not right!*"

"You don't know that she wants him back," Laci cried quietly. "She just said she wanted to see him."

"You think she spent all this money to come all this way because she just wants to," I made quote marks in the air, "*see* him?"

"Maybe," Laci said. "Who knows? You wouldn't even hear her out!"

"And I'm not going to hear her out," I told her, my voice shaking. "I'm also not going to sit around and do nothing like I did with Amber."

"You couldn't have done anything differently with Amber," Laci said gently.

"I don't want that woman anywhere near our house again," I said, ignoring her. "Do you understand me?"

She looked at me, her eyes still full of tears, not answering me. We stared at each other for what felt like a very, long time.

"Do you want to know what they named him?" she asked after we'd stared at each other in silence.

"*What?*"

"His name," she said quietly. "Don't you want to know his real name?"

"His name is *Dorito*."

"His real name," Laci went on, ignoring me, "is Rogelio. Rogelio Javier Escalante."

"His name," I shouted angrily, before turning and going out the front door, "is DORITO!"

~ ~ ~

"HI, DADDY!" DORITO waved as I walked into *Wilma's* where he and Tanner were finishing their lunch.

"Hey, buddy," I said, stooping down to wrap my arms around him. I lifted him off of his chair and squeezed him tightly, shutting my eyes as I held him.

"You made me mess up my picture!" he complained when I set him back down. He had been drawing on his plate with a French fry brush and ketchup paint. From what I could tell he had been making a dragon . . . or maybe it was a bat.

"Sorry," I said, keeping my hand on his shoulder. I finally let myself glance at Tanner who was eyeing me questioningly with a look of great concern on his face. I shook my head at him and looked away.

Tanner pushed his plate away and produced a set of headphones. He hooked them into his phone.

"Wanna watch that video again?" he asked Dorito.

"Okay," Dorito said, glaring at me, "since Daddy *ruined* my picture!"

Tanner punched away at some buttons while Dorito put the ear buds in. I didn't even ask what kind of inappropriate garbage he'd been exposing my child to.

"What's going on?" Tanner asked as soon as Dorito was engrossed in the video.

"His biological mother showed up," I said quietly.

"*What?*"

"You heard me."

"I thought he was an orphan!?"

"He was an orphan," I agreed. "He was found abandoned in a park and no one claimed him. That makes him an orphan."

"But I . . . I guess I thought his parents were dead."

"Apparently not," I said.

130

"What does she want?"

"Him," I said. "She wants *him.*"

"But you've had him for years! How can she just show up and expect to get him back?"

"She's not going to," I said. "I don't care what I have to do – I am *not* losing him."

I didn't add the word "too", but I knew we were both thinking it.

"How did she find you?"

"I have no idea," I said. "She just showed up at our door about an hour ago."

"She knocked on your door and said *'I want my kid back'*?" Tanner asked, incredulous.

"Well, she said she wanted to see him."

"She didn't say she wanted him back?"

"No," I admitted.

"What makes you think she wants him back?"

"Why else would she be here?" I asked. "What possible reason would she have for showing up on our doorstep?"

"Maybe she wants money."

"Oh, that's better."

"Or maybe she just wants to see him," Tanner shrugged, "like she said."

"Now you sound like Laci."

"Laci thinks she just wants to see him?"

I nodded.

"So why do you think there has to be more to it than that?"

"She came all the way from Mexico City!" I cried. "You don't do that just because you want to 'see' somebody!"

"What are you gonna do?"

"I'm not losing him," I said again.

"I don't see how she could possibly take him from you," Tanner said, shaking his head. "He's too old. You've had him for too long."

131

"Some judge might rule that she can have him back," I said worriedly. "I've heard of stupider things than that happening."

"I don't know," Tanner said, shaking his head skeptically. "I just can't see a judge giving Dorito to her after all this time."

"You don't think it's possible?"

He was quiet for a minute.

"You should get a lawyer," he finally said.

"I should move to Canada," I muttered.

"We're moving to Canada?" I heard Dorito ask. I looked down at him. Apparently his video was over.

"Let me have my phone," Tanner told him. Dorito handed it back to him.

"Why should we move to Canada?" Dorito asked, handing the phone across the table to Tanner. "So we can go salmon fishing?"

"What do you know about salmon fishing?" I asked, smiling at him.

"Everything," he said. "Tanner told me all about it. He's going to take me one day."

"Ahhhh," I said, nodding. "Do I get to go, too?"

"I guess."

"Gee, thanks."

By this time, Tanner had flipped open his phone and punched some buttons.

"Yes," he said after he'd held it up to his ear and waited for a minute. "I need to make an appointment with Madison . . . Yeah, I can hold."

"Who's Madison?" I asked.

"A friend of mine who's a lawyer."

"Is he good?"

"She."

"Madison's a she?"

"Very much so," Tanner grinned. I rolled my eyes.

"Is she good?"

"Very much so," he grinned again.

132

I shook my head and looked back down at Dorito. My hand was still on his shoulder and I gave him a squeeze.

"No," Tanner said after someone apparently came back on the line. "It can't wait until Friday. Could you tell her Tanner called? It's important . . . No, just tell her Tanner . . . Okay, thanks . . . Bye."

I turned and looked at him.

"She'll call me in a few minutes," Tanner assured me. Then he turned to Dorito. "You ready to blow this joint?"

"Yeah," Dorito nodded.

Tanner smiled and went to the counter to pay. Normally I would have jumped in and insisted on paying since he'd been feeding *my* kid, but I let Tanner get it because I still had my hand on Dorito and I didn't think I was ever going to be able to let him go.

I kept hold of Dorito's back and steered him out the door once Tanner had laid the tip on the table.

When we reached Tanner's truck he glanced down at Dorito and then asked me, "Don't you have a fun game on your phone that Dorito can play?"

"Uhhhh, I don't think so," I said.

"Yes, you do," Dorito argued.

"I do?"

"Uh-huh," he nodded. "You've got all *kinds* of games on there! You've got Tetris and Snake and-"

"Knock yourself out," I said, handing him the phone. Tanner opened the door to his truck and lifted Dorito from under my touch and set him in the seat. He slammed the door shut.

"I think you also need to call a private investigator," he said, glancing into the truck to make sure that Dorito was playing a game.

"A private investigator?"

"Yeah."

"Why?"

"You need to find out everything you can about this woman. For all you know, this is just some scam she runs on people all the time to extort money or something."

"You think that's what she's doing?" I asked, hopefully.

"Maybe," he shrugged.

"Should I really call a private eye?" I asked.

"Yes."

"How do I find one?"

"You're so lucky you know me," he said. He drew out his phone again and jabbed at it a few times with his finger.

"Grant? Hey, it's me . . . Yeah . . . No, no, I know. I've got something I need you to look into for me . . . I need a rundown on a woman from Mexico City . . ." He looked at me. "What's her name?"

"Savanna Escalante."

"Savanna Escalante," Tanner said into the phone and then he turned back to me. "Savanna got an 'h' on the end of it?"

"I have no idea."

"I have no idea," Tanner repeated and then listened. "She presumably flew up here from Mexico City within the past week. Yeah. Yeah – everything you can get. Financial records, criminal past. Dig up everything you can on her and her family. Any records of live births . . . everything."

He listened for another minute and then said, "By the way, this isn't for me. It's for my friend, David. He'll call you so you can give him whatever you find . . . and you can bill him directly." Tanner grinned at me. "Yeah . . . yeah, that's right . . . Okay . . . Yeah, okay . . . Talk to you soon . . . Thanks . . . Bye."

"Why do you have a private investigator in your contacts?" I asked when Tanner hung up.

"Doesn't everybody?" he smiled, and then he purposefully changed the subject to avoid answering my question. "Listen, this guy is good. If there's anything to find, he'll find it."

"Is this legal?" I asked.

"Yeah, it's legal," he said. "And that's why you're hiring Grant. Anything he finds he'll make sure it's admissible in court. He's a good guy – I promise you'll like him."

"And how do you know him?" I tried again.

"I just know him," Tanner shrugged.

"Why won't you tell me how you know him?"

"You got me," Tanner said, grinning again and throwing his hands up. "We're dating. We're actually making plans to move to San Francisco early next year."

"Very funny," I said as Tanner's phone rang.

"I told you she'd call me right back," he said, not even trying to hide the cocky look on his face as he looked at the display and opened his phone.

"Hey, Maddie," he said. They made small talk for a minute until he got to the point. "I've got a friend who needs help."

He listened to her response and then looked at his watch.

"Got it," he said. "We'll be there."

Twenty minutes later we were in downtown Cavendish. We approached a building that was about fifteen stories high, entered the lobby and took an elevator to the fourth floor. When we got out we saw a sign that welcomed us to the law offices of Snider and Snider. The secretary pointed us toward Madison's office, but as we started down the hall she called out, "Wait."

All three of us turned around and looked at her. She dropped her eyes down to Dorito.

"Do you like hot chocolate?" she asked him.

He nodded and she held out her hand.

"Why don't you and I go down to the snack bar and see what we can find? Would you like that?" He nodded. "They just broke out the hot chocolate last week. Yesterday they had marshmallows."

"Okay," he said eagerly. I tightened my grip on his shoulder and he looked up at me. "Can I?" he asked as an afterthought.

I nodded at him reluctantly, watched him take off with the secretary, and sighed. Dorito had never met a stranger. If Savanna Escalante ever wanted to swipe him from me one day, all she was going to have to do was wave a candy bar or video game in front of his nose and he was going to be gone.

We started back down the hall to Madison's office. The door was open and as we entered, a tall brunette rose from behind a desk and crossed the room to give Tanner a warm embrace. I briefly wondered if he'd ever dated a girl who wasn't a knockout.

"Good to see you, Tanner," she said.

"You too, Maddie," he nodded. Then he turned to me. "This is David Holland."

"Mr. Holland," she said, extending her hand. "Very nice to meet you. I'm Madison Snider."

"Nice to meet you," I said, shaking her hand. "Call me David."

She nodded.

"And since you're friends with Tanner," she said, "you may call me Madison."

She pointed to a cluster of leather chairs surrounding a coffee table. "Let's sit," she suggested. After we'd gotten settled she looked directly at me and said, "What can I do for you?"

I told her the whole story. She listened carefully, asking questions, taking notes. When I mentioned that I'd hired a private investigator she asked who it was.

"Grant Larson," Tanner told her and she nodded her approval.

After I was finished telling her everything, she steepled her hands in front of her, apparently deep in thought.

"There are a couple of things we can do," Madison finally said. "Why don't I run down your options and then we can talk about how you want to proceed."

"Okay," I nodded. "Sounds good."

"A restraining order?" Laci cried after I'd gotten home that afternoon. "You can't file a restraining order against her!"

"I can," I said. "And I did."

"David! How can you do that to this poor woman? She's been away from her child for all this time and now she's finally found him and she wants to meet him! She just wants to see him and make sure he's okay! Why can't you let her do that? I don't understand how you can be so cruel!"

"You think I'm being cruel?"

"Yes," she nodded. "I do. I think it's cruel to not let her see him."

"Do you know what's the first thing I think about every morning when I wake up?" I asked her.

She looked at me for a long moment and then finally nodded. Her eyes glistened with tears.

"I wonder if she's awake yet or if she's still sleeping. I wonder if she's going to have a good day . . . if she's happy. I wonder if she smiles or talks." I heard my voice break. "I wonder if she thinks about me . . . if she even remembers me."

"David-" Laci said, reaching a hand toward me.

"And you don't even care!" I shouted, pulling away from her.

"I care!" she protested. "I miss her too!"

"Oh, yeah," I said. "I can tell you were really torn up about it."

"Why?" she yelled back. "Just because I didn't mope around and refuse to have anything to do with anybody? Just because I manage to get out of bed every day and *function?* You think that means I don't miss her?"

I glared at her.

"We have to move on with our lives," Laci said. "We have other

137

children to worry about."

"But apparently Dorito's not one of them," I said. "As long as you've got Lily, that's really all you care about."

"You know that's not true," she whispered in an appalled voice.

"What I know is true is that this woman has just waltzed into our lives and is threatening to take away what little we have left and you don't seem worried about it at all!"

"Look," she said. "I wish none of this had happened, but it has. Savanna's found us and she wants to meet Dorito. She has a right to see him – she's his *mother*."

"You're his mother," I said evenly, holding her gaze.

"David," she said softly. "I know that you're scared. I know that what happened with Amber has made you afraid that you're going to lose Dorito too, but that's not what's going on here. She just wants to *meet* him."

"Let me ask you something," I said. She nodded. "Let's pretend that when that doorbell rang, you'd opened up the door and there was – let's say there was a detective standing there. He'd been investigating the hospital where Gabby was born . . ."

I saw pain flash across Laci's face at the mention of Gabby's name, but I went on.

"So let's say there was some big cover-up. Gabby wasn't stillborn after all. Gabby was a healthy little girl who got whisked away from us and . . ." my mind searched desperately for a scenario, "and sold to some sort of black-market baby ring or something."

"We held her!" Laci argued, tears now flowing down her cheeks. "You know Gabby died."

"Yes, I *know* Gabby died!" I shouted. "I'm trying to make a point here. So *what if*? What if you found out that Gabby was still alive. What would you do?"

I was hurting her, but I couldn't stop. I plowed ahead.

"Would you just want to *meet* her? *'Hi, Gabby! I'm your real mom. I just wanted to meet you and pat you on the head. Well, it looks like you've got yourself a nice life, so now I'm gonna leave you alone and not bother you and your new family anymore.'* Are you honestly going to sit here and tell me that that's what you'd do?"

Laci didn't say anything. She just glared at me and wiped away angry tears with the back of her hand.

"No," I answered for her. "You'd want to get her back. You'd do anything you could to have her back again. And that's exactly how this woman feels."

"This is different," Laci protested.

"HOW? How is this different?"

She didn't answer me . . . I don't think she could.

"She's going to go after Dorito," I insisted. "She's going to do whatever she can to get him back."

Laci shook her head at me.

"Yes, she is," I argued. "And I'm going to do whatever it takes to keep that from happening."

~ ~ ~

BY SATURDAY, GRANT, my private investigator, had managed to track down Savanna – she was staying at a hotel downtown. I shared this information with Madison who, in turn, called me on Monday night and told me that Savanna had been served with a temporary restraining order. She told me that a hearing was going to be held soon on the order and that – in the meantime – if Savanna tried to contact us or come within two hundred yards of any of us, I was to call the police.

Wednesday morning, Dorito was at school and Laci had taken Lily to speech therapy. I was home alone when the doorbell rang. I answered it to find a man standing on my front porch.

The first thing I noticed about him was his gold badge with black letters that was attached to his light, brown dress shirt. The badge read: N. Daly. He had on dark brown pants that had black stripes running up each leg and that were being held up by a shiny, black belt (which matched his shiny, black boots). The shiny, black belt was also holding a set of keys, a nightstick, pepper spray, a flashlight, a radio, handcuffs and a 9mm Glock. His cap pronounced that he was a Deputy Sheriff and (just so you know), when someone like this shows up on your doorstep, it's never a good thing. *Never.*

"Are you David Holland?" he asked.

"Yes."

"I have papers to serve you, sir," he said, handing me a bulky envelope.

"What is this?" I asked, taking it from him.

"I have no idea, sir. I don't read 'em, I just serve 'em." He wrote something down in a notebook. Then he touched the brim of his hat and said, "Have a good day."

"Thank you," I said vaguely, as he turned and walked down the stairs. I closed the door and looked at the envelope in my hands. I slit it open with my finger, pulled a thick set of papers out of it, unfolded them, and began skimming the pages.

**David Holland,
Petitioner, v. Savanna
Evita Torres Escalante,
Respondent-Mother.**

———————————

**Savanna Evita
Torres Escalante,
Counterpetitioner v.
David Holland and Laci
Cline Holland,
Counterrespondent.**

No. SD 8011983.

**Motion to Set
Aside Judgment.**

Timothy R. Beckham, Carlos Riojas, for Respondent S.E.T.E..
Caleb S. Michaels, for Petitioner Kawartha County Juvenile Office.
Alden C. McClure, Madison Snider for Petitioners D.H. & L.C.H..

Savanna Evita Torres Escalante ("Mother"), a citizen of Mexico, hereby moves to set aside the judgment granting a petition for termination of parental rights ("TPR") and subsequent adoption of her minor son, Doroteo Alano Fernandez ("Child"), filed by David Holland and Laci Cline Holland (collectively, "Respondents"), and entered by the Circuit Court of Kawartha County. There are four bases for this motion. Through no fault of her own, Mother was unlawfully prevented from participating in prior proceedings. Mother had no knowledge of prior proceedings . . .

It went on for *eleven* pages:

> The court found that Mother "abandoned" Child, as used
> in sections 102.065(7) and 113.096.4(2)(b) . . . recognition of
> foreign adoption . . . the court stated that Mother had no
> contact with Child nor attempted to communicate with him
> from the time he was found . . . not a party to original
> hearing . . . excusable neglect . . . Biological father, ("Father")
> did without lawful authority, physically asport Child without
> consent from Mother (Model Penal Code § 512.1) . . .
> Additionally, nothing in the record indicates that Mother knew
> how to contact Child or where to find him either before or after
> he was placed with Respondents . . . father further denied
> mother the opportunity to contest adoption through physical
> and psychological means . . . judgments are void . . . it is of
> course true that the [adoption] statute is to be liberally construed
> with a view to promoting the best interests of the child, but such
> liberal construction is obviously not to be extended to the
> question of when the natural parents may be divested of their
> rights to the end that all legal relationship between them and their
> child shall cease and determine . . . [I]t must always be borne in
> mind that the rights of natural parents to the custody and
> possession of their children are among the highest of natural
> rights[.] . . .

There it was – my worst fear – right before my eyes in black and
white.

Savanna Escalante was trying to reverse our adoption of Dorito.

142

~ ~ ~

TANNER WAS AT school and I was planning on leaving him a message, so he surprised me when he answered his phone.

"Yo," he said.

"She wants Dorito."

There was a long, long pause.

"Are you sure?" he finally asked.

"A sheriff's deputy just showed up at my front door and served me with papers," I said shortly. "How much more '*sure*' do you want me to be?"

"Do you want me to call Madison?" he asked, ignoring my rudeness.

"I already called her."

"What did she say?"

"I'm meeting her at her office in thirty minutes."

"Do you want me to go with you?" he asked.

"Aren't you teaching?"

"I'm inflating basketballs," he said. "Do you want me to go with you?"

"Yes."

"I'll meet you there," he said and I called Laci next.

"You still think Savanna Escalante's just some poor woman who's been misunderstood and who wants nothing more than a few moments with her long, lost son?" I asked her.

I got just about as long of a pause from her as I had from Tanner.

"What's going on?" she finally asked quietly.

"Oh, nothing much," I said acidly. "She's just trying to get the adoption overturned so she can take him back to Mexico and we'll never get to see him again."

"She wouldn't do that."

"Oh, *really?* Then why did a sheriff 's deputy just served me with

143

papers?"

I got another long pause and then she said, "I'll . . . I'll be home in a few minutes."

"Don't do me any favors," I snapped and I hung up the phone.

Twenty minutes later I was waiting in the lobby of Madison's office with Tanner.

"Let me see what you got," Tanner asked. I handed the papers to him.

"Why does it say Doroteo *Alano Fernandez?*" he wanted to know after he'd only been looking at it for a minute.

"It was the name the orphanage assigned him with after he was *abandoned in the park* and nobody came forward to tell us what his real name was."

"So, it's just like . . . made up?"

"Basically," I nodded.

"You don't know his birthday either," Tanner realized slowly. "You celebrate it in January, but you don't know that that's when he was really born, do you?"

I shook my head.

"I wonder when it is," Tanner said, more to himself than to me. I glared at him and he quit talking.

Eventually, Madison stepped out into the hall.

"David?" she said, motioning us back.

We went back into her office and I handed her the stack of papers.

"What does it mean?" Tanner asked after Madison had finished perusing the document and looked back up at us.

"She's entering a motion with the Circuit Court to set aside the ruling on your adoption petition," she told me, confirming what I already had figured.

144

"On what grounds?" Tanner asked.

"They're claiming that she never consented to the adoption."

"He was abandoned in a park!" I cried. "When she deserted him that made him an orphan and he was adoptable. We didn't *need* her consent."

"She's claiming *she* didn't desert him," Madison said, shaking her head. "She's claiming her *husband* left him in the park without her knowledge. Essentially she's claiming that he was kidnapped."

"Kidnapped?"

"Yes. By her husband. She's contending that he kept the child from her without her consent and then refused to tell her where the boy was. She claims she was abused and oppressed by her husband and was not able to freely pursue searching for the child until her husband recently became ill and subsequently died. She began searching for the child immediately after her husband passed away."

"Does she have a case?" I asked. She hesitated and I kept looking at her – waiting for her to say something that would unknot my stomach.

She didn't.

"If she can prove that the child was kidnapped, the motion potentially could be granted."

"But David and Laci have had him for over four years," Tanner protested. "He's never known any other parents . . ."

"There's no question that returning him to his biological mother may not be in his best interest, but if she can prove that she didn't abandon him and that she never consented to the adoption . . . it may not matter. A parent's right to raise her children is one of the oldest fundamental liberty interests recognized by the United States Supreme Court."

"They can't take Dorito away," Tanner said, shaking his head. "It's not right."

"When her husband took the child from her, he committed a crime," Madison said carefully. "Unfortunately, when a crime has been committed, things often don't turn out 'right'. Almost always, somebody gets hurt."

145

"Can't you do something?" Tanner asked.

She looked at him for a moment, and then at me.

"Mr. Holland," she finally began.

"David," I reminded her.

"David. Let me explain something to you."

"Okay."

"My husband and I are partners here at this law firm. It's just the two of us. We handle everything from divorce and custody cases to DUIs and minor traffic violations. We also do our fair share of real-estate deals, wills, setting up trust funds, that sort of thing."

I nodded.

"My husband takes most of the cases involving criminal offenses and I do most of the family law cases. We don't always defer to each other, but for the most part, I get the custody and visitation cases. Okay?"

"Okay."

"So I've had a lot of experience in this area."

I nodded again.

"If this was a typical case, I would agree to represent you right now, but . . ."

"But what?"

"This is not a typical case."

I may have nodded one more time.

"Honestly," she went on, "I don't even know of any similar situations that could be referred to. I'm sure there are some – somewhere – but I have no idea where I'd even begin. Furthermore, this motion is only addressing the adoption that was granted at the state level – it doesn't even touch the original adoption in Mexico itself. I have no experience in the international laws that would be at play here and that makes me very hesitant to offer you my assistance."

"What am I supposed to do?" I asked in a weak voice.

"Have you ever heard of Reanna Justice?" Madison asked.

I knew I'd heard the name before, but it took me a minute to

146

remember where.

"The frozen embryo case?" I finally asked.

"Yes."

"What frozen embryo case?" Tanner wanted to know. Madison turned toward him.

"It made national headlines about five years ago," she explained. "An infertile couple in Idaho purchased four frozen embryos from a fertility clinic in West Virginia. They hired a woman from Michigan to act as a surrogate. All four embryos were implanted and three of them developed. Two healthy boys and one healthy girl were carried to term."

She glanced at me and then back to Tanner.

"About two months before the babies were due, a couple from Canada came forward and claimed that the embryos were theirs and that they'd never given up custody of them. They sued everybody involved . . . the couple from Idaho, the surrogate mother and the fertility clinic. DNA tests revealed that the babies were indeed the biological offspring of the couple from Canada. They wanted five million dollars in damages and full custody."

She turned and faced me now. "Reanna Justice was the attorney for the couple from Idaho. She's the one you need to hire."

"She's an attorney," Tanner interjected, "and her last name is *Justice?*"

"Pretty sweet, huh?" Madison asked, smiling at him. "And I'm stuck here working at Snider and Snider."

"But the Idaho couple *lost*, didn't they?" I protested. "Didn't the biological parents get those babies?"

"Yes," Madison admitted, "and they were awarded two million dollars from the fertility clinic, but there's no way that that Idaho couple was ever going to be granted custody. Those embryos were sold illegally. Granted, the Idaho couple didn't *know* that, but there was no chance that any court was going to award them custody instead of the biological parents when no one had even laid hands on the infants yet. It was a given from day one that those embryos were going to be awarded to their biological parents as soon as they were born. No lawyer in the world was going to stop that from happening."

I think she could tell that I wasn't too impressed.

"That case should never have even made it to court," she explained, leaning toward me. "The only reason there even *was* a trial was because they hired Reanna Justice as their lawyer. I don't know of anybody else who could have gotten it as far as she did."

"So you think she's good," I stated.

"She's the best," Madison said. "Plus I bet she'd love to sink her teeth into this. Like I said, this is a really unusual situation. If you don't want to lose your son, you'll get her on retainer right away."

~ ~ ~

LACI AND I had a knock-down, drag-out that night after the kids were in bed. It was a good thing that Dorito was a sound sleeper and that Lily was deaf.

"She's his mother!" Laci yelled at me. "She should be allowed to see her child!"

"Why don't we just work out a visitation schedule with her?" I shouted back. "Every other weekend with one week at Christmas and then a month in the summer? How's that sound? Or maybe we could let her move in with us or . . . Oh, no! I've got it! Why don't we *move down there with her?* That's what you really think we should do, isn't it?"

Laci glared at me.

"She is *not* taking my son from me," I told her. "Do you understand? I will do anything . . . *anything* to keep that woman from getting my son."

"She just wants to see him . . ."

"Yeah," I yelled. "That's why she's hired a lawyer! That's why she's trying to get the adoption overturned and why she's trying to get her parental rights back!"

"She hired a lawyer because you backed her into a corner!" Laci cried. "The only reason she even *went* to an attorney in the first place was because she wanted to see if he could get her permission to meet Dorito somehow! He decided to represent her pro bono and he's the one that convinced her that they should try for full custody. It wasn't her idea. None of this even would have happened if you'd just let her see him!"

"*You've been talking to her?*" I asked, stunned.

"Yes, I've been talking to her! I feel sorry for her!"

"You can't talk to her!" I yelled. "Our attorney specifically said that we're to have no communication with her, whatsoever."

"*Your* attorney."

"What?"

"I said 'Your attorney'. She's *your* attorney . . . not *my* attorney. I'm not keeping her from seeing Dorito . . . *you* are. I think it's heartless that you won't let her see him and I'm not going to be a part of it."

"You're taking her side on this?" I asked, staring at her in disbelief. "You're helping her?"

"I'm not helping her – I'm just trying to do what's right!"

I set my jaw and fixed my eyes on her. The next time I spoke, I didn't yell.

"You are not to talk to her again," I said, my voice controlled and even. "Do you understand?"

Laci was – *we* were – very conservative in our beliefs about the roles of a man and woman in a marriage. If Laci and I disagreed on something, we tried to talk it out and work out a solution. But if we couldn't come to a mutual agreement about something, then the final decision was up to me. I realize that in this time of women's rights and equality, this belief might sound archaic, but – Biblically – we believed that the man was appointed as head of his wife just as Christ is head of the Church.

(I would like to take this opportunity here to point out that I didn't take my responsibilities lightly, nor did I ever take unfair advantage of my position. When we'd been living in Mexico and Laci had been diagnosed with cancer, I'd insisted that we return to the United States for her treatments – even though she had fought me tooth and nail. That was the *only* time I had ever used the "A-Man-is-the-Head-of-His-Wife" card.)

I was about to play it again, though.

"*Do you understand?*" I demanded sternly when she didn't answer.

She glared at me, her face full of hatred, but she finally gave me the slightest of nods.

"Good," I said, and I turned around and stormed out of our bedroom.

150

I went into the office and briefly surveyed the full-sized couch that was in there. This was the couch where Lily had snuggled on my lap and first said the word Daddy . . . where Charlotte had told her mother that she was pregnant . . . where I had taught Amber how to play chess . . . where Laci and I had made up after I'd found out that she and Tanner had once loved each other . . . the couch where Dorito had sobbed against my chest after Amber had left us.

Now, I didn't pull out the hidden mattress, but I did grab one of the pillows from the closet and I tucked a sheet around the cushions of the couch. Then I laid a second sheet and two blankets down and tucked them in as well. Finally, I pulled back the top sheet and the blankets, took off my slippers and bathrobe, and then I lay down – in the bed that I had made for myself.

~ ~ ~

IF TANNER AND I had not already been planning on going fishing the next day, I probably would have called him and begged him to take me – the thought of spending the entire day with Laci set my teeth on edge. He picked me up before the sun was up, as planned, and I strapped a groggy Dorito into the back of his truck before we pulled away.

"What did Laci say?" Tanner asked quietly, once Dorito had resumed his gentle snoring.

"About what?" I asked shortly.

"About the United Nation's summit on the world's economy," he said, sardonically, cutting his eyes at me.

I glanced back to make sure Dorito was asleep.

"She thinks this is all my fault," I said.

"How's she figure that?"

"She thinks if I had just let Savanna see him, none of this would have happened. She thinks we should just let Savanna see him whenever she wants."

"She does?"

"Yeah. If she had her way about it we'd move down to Mexico and live with Savanna. One big, happy family."

"Oh, she would not!" Tanner exclaimed.

"Yes she would!" I insisted. "You know what a bleeding heart she is! Plus she's just been looking for an excuse to move back to Mexico."

"Laci wants to move back to Mexico?"

"Oh, yeah," I nodded. "She's just waiting for *God* to tell me that that's what He wants us to do and then we're moving."

"Are you really thinking about moving back?" he asked quietly.

"No, I'm not thinking about moving back!" I hissed, stealing another glance at Dorito. "I'm *never* going back to Mexico! Especially now that I know Dorito's mother lives there! I'm gonna keep him as far away from

152

her as I possibly can."

"But, Laci-"

"Laci can just get over it," I snapped.

He was silent for a moment.

"Maybe you could talk with this lady and tell her that she can see him if she promises to drop everything."

"Then it'll look like we think she really *does* have a right to see him. It's too late to go down that road now."

"But maybe if you and Laci try to-"

"Tanner?" I interrupted.

"What?"

"Can we not talk about this?"

He didn't say anything, but he nodded his head slightly.

"I just . . . I'm sorry. I just don't want to talk about Savanna or lawsuits or Laci or anything," I explained. "I just want to go fishing."

"Okay."

"I'm not trying to be rude."

"No," he said, shaking his head. "No problem. I get it."

I felt myself relax.

"Thanks," I said, leaning back against the headrest.

"Nothing's gonna help you get your mind off your troubles," he said, giving me a sly smile, "like getting out-fished by the Master."

It was a day filled with Dorito's endless chatter, perch, walleyes, and bass. I stretched it out as long as I could, offering to buy lunch and then later dinner just so that I wouldn't have to go home. When Tanner finally dropped us off that night, he came in to say hello to Laci and Lily. Laci was polite to Tanner, but the tension between the two of us was so thick that it was almost palpable.

"We should go again, tomorrow," I suggested as Tanner got ready to leave.

"Sure," he shrugged. (Tanner had never been one to turn down an opportunity to go fishing.) "Want me to pick you up after lunch?"

"No," I said, shaking my head. "Let's get up there about the same time we did this morning.

"Okay," he said slowly and I could feel Laci's eyes boring holes through the back of my head.

"We're going again?" Dorito shouted, jumping into the air and clapping his hands.

"No," I said, quickly. "You're not going this time."

"Why can't I?" he whined.

"Because you have church."

"Why don't *you* have church?" he wanted to know.

"Because I'm going fishing," I told him, and I slept on the couch that night, too.

Tanner and I spent all day Sunday at Cross Lake again. He didn't mention one word about Dorito, the adoption hearing, the restraining order, or the fact that I was skipping church.

Neither did I.

When he dropped me off that evening he joined us for pizza (pretending he didn't notice the fact that neither Laci and nor I were speaking to one another).

After we'd eaten, Tanner followed me up to my office to get a duck stamp that I'd purchased for him a few days earlier.

"Here ya go," I said, handing it to him. He took it from me and put it in his wallet. Then he picked up a foam ball from my desk and shot it toward the plastic basketball goal that was mounted on the back of the door.

The ball almost made it through the net, but hit left and bounced off

154

the door and rolled toward the couch. Tanner went to retrieve it and that's when he noticed the pillow, sheets and blankets that were there.

He looked up at me.

"Don't start," I warned.

"I didn't say a word," he said, holding up his hand. He sat down on my couch/bed and tossed the ball back and forth from one oversized hand to the other.

"What time's the hearing tomorrow?" he asked after a minute. (The next day was the initial hearing about the restraining order.)

"Ten," I answered.

"You still going?"

I nodded. Madison had assured me that I didn't need to be there, but I had insisted that I wanted to go.

"Do you guys want me to watch Lily or something?" he offered. "I could take the day off if you need me to."

"No," I said, shaking my head.

"You're taking her with you?"

"No," I said tightly. "Laci's not going."

He looked at me for a long moment.

"I'm going to get a sub," he finally said pulling out his phone, "so I can go with you."

"You don't have to do that," I said, shaking my head.

"Is there a reason you don't want me there?" he asked, his phone poised in midair.

"Well, no . . ."

"Would you rather go alone?"

"No," I admitted.

"Then shut up," he said, poking at his phone and then holding a finger up to his lips. "I'm trying to sound sick."

~ ~ ~

SOMEHOW MADISON HAD gotten in touch with Reanna Justice on Friday afternoon and not only convinced her to take my case, but to fly in on time for the restraining order hearing on Monday. I met her right before the bailiff called our case.

"Nice to meet you," she said briskly, shaking my hand.

"This is my friend, Tanner," I said.

"Nice to meet you," she said to him, just as briskly.

"Nice to meet *you*," he answered, shaking her hand and holding it much longer than what I thought was necessary.

Unbelievable. I shot him what I hoped was a disdainful look.

"What?" he whispered innocently as we sat down directly behind Reanna and Madison. "I can't help it if you've got *hot* attorneys."

I did my best to glare at him, wondering if he had any idea how thankful I was that he and his sense of humor were there with me. The bailiff called the courtroom to order.

"The circuit court of Kawartha County is now in session," he announced. "The Honorable Judge Trafford Goebeler presiding."

I looked at Tanner and Tanner looked at me.

Trafford Goebeler? I mouthed discretely at Tanner. Simultaneously (and not so discretely), Tanner whispered, *"Trafford Goebeler?"*

I don't think Trafford Goebeler heard him, but Reanna sure did. She turned around and glared at him, her eyes shooting daggers.

"Sorry," Tanner whispered contritely, sitting back.

I had a file folder on my lap. I wrote on it and showed it to Tanner:

I think she's very attracted to you.

He grinned at me.

The attorneys stated their names and who they were representing for

156

the records and then dove right into their arguments about the restraining order. Savanna sat at another table with two men. Once of them was clearly her attorney – he had introduced himself as Timothy R. Beckham. I didn't know if the other guy was an attorney too or if he was just a translator, but he spent the entire time whispering quietly into Savanna's ear.

Just like Madison had predicted (and why she'd told me I didn't really even need to be there today), the judge decided to leave the temporary restraining order in place until the hearing on Savanna's request to set aside the adoption and the termination of her parental rights.

"Are there any other matters to be brought before the court at this time?" Judge Goebeler asked.

"Yes, your honor," Beckham said. "We are requesting that the child immediately be returned to Mexico City under the mandates of the Hague Convention."

"*What?*" Reanna cried, clearly taken aback. "Your Honor, that's absurd."

"Your Honor," Beckham argued, "under the Hague Convention, the courts are required in cases like this to promptly return a child to their country of habitual residence to preserve the status quo arrangement that existed before the removal of the child from the country."

Reanna was shuffling frantically through a stack of papers. I glanced at Tanner, worriedly.

"Your Honor," Reanna said, putting the papers down and looking up at him, "under Article 13b, the court's mandatory obligation to return a child to his country of habitual residence is changed to a discretionary obligation if there's evidence there is grave risk that the child's return would expose the child to physical or psychological harm or otherwise place the child in an intolerable situation. This child is almost nine years old and has resided with Mr. and Mrs. Holland – for all intents and purposes – for almost five years. During that time, he has never known any other parents. He is a well-adjusted, happy young man who has lived

157

in this country for over three years. He is currently enrolled in the same public school that he has attended since kindergarten. Furthermore, the child is not even aware that a custody dispute has developed. To unnecessarily make him aware of this fact at this time would be psychologically devastating to him – not to even *mention* the trauma associated with removing him from his home."

"Your Honor," Beckham interjected. "The primary intention of the Convention is to preserve whatever custody arrangement existed immediately before an alleged wrongful removal or retention."

"Your Honor," Reanna said, "the child *is* currently in the same custody arrangement he was in before he was brought to this country. The respondent was not exercising custody at the time of the removal. Prior to the child's removal from the country he had already been adopted by the petitioner. Furthermore, before returning to the United States, the defendant filed an orphan petition with the BCIS. This petition was approved and the child was issued an immigrant visa after which he accompanied his family upon their return to the U.S. Since that time, he has been considered a lawful, permanent resident of the United States. Mr. and Mrs. Holland had legal custody for a full year before returning to the United States."

"Again, Your Honor, the Hague Convention provisions for children who have been abducted or wrongfully retained-"

"Objection, your Honor. There is no evidence that an abduction even occurred."

"The reason for our original motion, your Honor, is to show that the child was abducted from his biological mother and withheld from her without her consent or knowledge. Immediately prior to this, the mother had legal custody in Mexico-"

"Your Honor, the Hague Convention only makes provisions for children to be returned to their country of habitual residence when they were abducted to a foreign country. This alleged abduction took place two years before the child was removed from the country. The Hague

158

Convention clearly does not apply here."

The judge had finally heard enough.

"The Court rules that the provisions of the Hague Convention do not apply in this case." He looked over his glasses at Beckham. "Furthermore, the Court finds that the child's return at this time to Mexico may expose him to psychological harm. Request denied."

Reanna whirled around, looked up to the ceiling, and mouthed something that looked like *Thank you, God.*

"Anything else?"

"Nothing at this time, Your Honor," Beckham said.

"Yes, Your Honor," Reanna said.

"Go ahead."

"Your Honor, we request that the date for the hearing for the respondent's motion to set aside the TPR and adoption rulings be moved to a later date. Due to the unusual circumstances regarding this case, we anticipate needing considerably more time to prepare than what is currently being provided."

The judge rifled through some papers in his hands.

"How much time does counsel need to prepare?"

"Your Honor, we request twelve weeks."

Judge Goebeler looked at Beckham. "Any objections?"

"Your Honor, Mrs. Escalante is in this country at her own expense and is currently away from her other biological children. It is our desire to resolve this matter as quickly as possible so that her entire family may be reunited at home. We are prepared to begin arguments in three weeks as scheduled and request that the date of the hearing not be changed."

Judge Goebeler peered over his glasses at both attorneys.

"I'm assuming you're each proceeding with independent DNA testing?"

"Yes, Your Honor," Reanna said.

"Yes, Your Honor," Beckham said.

"When do you expect the results?"

"Next week, Your Honor," Beckham answered.

"Three to four weeks, Your Honor," Reanna stated.

The judge rubbed his hands across his lips in thought. Then he consulted his calendar.

"Opening arguments will begin in eight weeks," he finally decided. "Anything else?"

"No, Your Honor."

"No, Your Honor."

"Very well," he said. "We'll reconvene in ten minutes."

I looked at Reanna as the judge got up and left the courtroom.

"Are we done?"

"Yes."

"But he said we were going to reconvene."

"He meant *court* will reconvene," Madison explained. "To hear the other cases that are on the docket?"

"Oh," I said.

"Idiot," Tanner mumbled.

"Right. Like you knew that," I shot at him.

Reanna looked at both of us as if we were eight years old.

"It's good, right?" I asked her. "Everything went good?"

"Yes," she said. Then she looked at Madison, "He threw me when he brought up the Hague Convention. I never expected that."

"That's because it was a stupid move," Madison said. "He's just grasping at straws."

Reanna looked at me. "You'd have been screwed if the judge had gone along with that request to return your son to Mexico."

I took a deep breath.

"The longer he's with you – in this country – the better our chances are going to be," she went on. "Public sentiment down there is much more likely to swing their way. Keeping it here, I'm pretty sure that the public support is going to be with us."

"Public support?"

"CNN, editorials . . . all that."

"This is going to be in the *news?*"

"You'd better hope it's going to be in the news," she said, stuffing some papers into her briefcase. "Judges can't help but pay attention to that sort of thing . . . it may be their job to be impartial and do what's right, but part of them wants to do whatever's going to make them most popular in the eyes of the public. And I imagine that the overwhelming majority of public support will be on our side."

"But I don't want this in the news!" I cried. I glanced at Madison for help. She gave me a small shrug.

"You just said it yourself," I pointed out to Reanna, "Dorito doesn't even know about this! If the press gets ahold of it everybody's going to know!"

"*Dorito?*" she exclaimed.

"It's . . . it's a nickname," I stammered.

She stared at me with a perplexed look on her face, then she said, "Don't you *dare* call him that in front of the judge."

"Okay," I said, meekly.

She shook her head as if to clear her mind.

"Anyway," she went on, "You need to pull out all the stops on this one. It's bad enough that your wife isn't sitting here by your side crying big, fat crocodile tears-"

"I'm here," Tanner pointed out. Madison smiled at him. Reanna ignored him.

"We need to do whatever we can to influence this judge," she advised.

"No," I insisted, shaking my head. "I don't want this in the news."

She looked at me for a long time.

"You're tying my hands," she said.

"You can do this without the media," I said. "I know you can."

"You don't need to suck up to me, Mr. Holland," she said. "I'm not the judge. You hired me – I won't leak it to the press if you're sure that's what you want. I just want to make sure that you're fully aware of the implications of your decisions."

I nodded. "I'm aware."

"Fine," she said, snapping her briefcase shut. "If we get really desperate, we'll talk about it again."

"What about him?" I asked, nodding toward Beckham. "Can we stop him from alerting the press?"

"I don't think we need to worry about it," she said. "I truly don't think public sentiment will be on his side and I suspect he feels the same way – that's probably one of the reasons he wanted to get this case out of the country if possible. I don't think he's going to alert the press, but – if he does decide to – there's not a lot we can do to stop him. Because Doroteo is a minor, the media won't be allowed to release his name. You and your wife, however, would be fair game."

"You said *'if we get desperate'*," I reminded her. "What do you think our chances are right now?"

"I never try to predict how a case is going to turn out."

"I could lose him," I said, flatly.

"Let's not get ahead of ourselves, okay?"

I nodded.

"What about the hearing date?" I asked. "He ruled closer to the time that we asked for . . . that's good, right?"

"Yes," she said. "Everything that's happened so far bodes very well for us. I think we're off to a good start."

"So, what do we do now?" I asked.

"Go home and enjoy your family," she said. "I'll see you in eight weeks."

That afternoon, when I got home, Laci spoke to me for the first time since Friday night.

162

"What happened?" she asked.

"If you wanted to know so badly," I said shortly, "maybe you should have been there with me."

She stared at me icily for a moment and then turned on her heel and left the room.

And except for obligatory conversations that we had to have with one another about the house or the kids or the dog, we didn't try to talk to each other again for eight weeks.

~ ~ ~

ONE MONTH BEFORE the hearing, Reanna flew into town again. She wanted to meet with me in Madison's office the next morning. Tanner offered to take another day off of work to come along.

"I got the distinct impression that she wanted you to *not* be there."

"Are you sure?" Tanner asked, a smug look on his face.

"Pretty sure," I nodded. Normally I would have welcomed Tanner and his attempts to keep my mind off of my troubles, but Reanna wanted to go over my testimony with me and I needed to concentrate on what we were doing. I really didn't want to screw up in the courtroom.

When I arrived at Madison's office, Reanna was already there in a conference room, clicking away on her laptop.

"Hi," she said, barely looking up.

"Hi," I said back.

"Give me one second," she said. I sat down and waited for her to finish. She tapped away at her keyboard for a few more minutes and then closed her computer up and looked at me.

"The DNA results are in," she told me.

"He's hers," I said. "Isn't he?"

She nodded.

"And your P.I. sent me his report," she added. "You got a copy, right?"

I nodded.

"Okay," she said. "So, I guess you saw that there really wasn't a lot in there that's going to help our case either. It looks like she's pretty much been telling the truth, as far as I can tell."

I sighed.

"But, on a more positive note, all the paperwork and everything that was done on your end looks great. It's really good that you pursued a state adoption after you brought him home. She's gonna have to overturn that adoption first, then any appeals we file, and then even if she gets through all that she'll still have to go through the same thing with the adoption in Mexico. Even if she keeps winning, we can keep this thing tied up in the courts for years."

"I don't-"

"I know you don't want this thing hanging over your head for years," she said. "I'm just saying."

I nodded and sighed.

"They're apparently only planning on calling two witnesses," Reanna told me.

"Who?"

"One of them is a psychologist – Zoe Walker. I've heard of her before. No doubt she's going to testify that Savanna was so abused by her husband that she didn't believe she had any options available to her once he took Doroteo away."

"Who else is going to testify?" I asked. "Savanna?"

"No," Reanna said, shaking her head. I don't think they'll want her to take the stand."

"Why not?"

"Because then I'll be able to bring up questions like how did Doroteo get rickets? Weren't they feeding him properly? Obviously they weren't taking good care of him . . . stuff like that."

"Oh," I said. "Who's it going to be then?"

"Her oldest son. Claudio."

Her oldest son. Dorito's brother.

"Why do they want him to testify?" I asked.

"I suspect that he's going to corroborate Savanna's story that her husband was abusive. They're going to try to prove that the father not only took Doroteo without Savanna's knowledge, but that he prevented her from looking for him."

She looked at me for a moment.

"Once an abducted child has been found," she went on, "they're

165

naturally returned to their parent. Beckham is going to contend that this is really no different than any other kidnapping situation."

"Do you think I could lose him?" I asked in a small voice.

"It's possible that the judge may rule to set aside the adoption if they can convince him that Savanna never had a chance to contest the original rulings."

"What are we going to do?" I asked anxiously

"We're going to prove that she had a chance."

Reanna wasn't going to be asking me a lot of questions herself and I felt completely ready for that part of my testimony, but Beckham was going to get to question me as well. There was no telling what he might throw at me and Reanna wanted me to be prepared for anything. We spent the next few hours practicing what I should say when Beckham examined me.

"Police records show that you placed a 911 call last year because you could not find Doroteo?" she asked, pretending to be Beckham. "Apparently he ran away from home?"

"No," I said. "He put a magnet on the TV and it messed the screen all up. He didn't know that it would be alright once you turned the TV off and on again. He thought he'd ruined it and he got scared . . . so he hid in his closet. We couldn't find him – we looked everywhere for him. We went up and down the neighborhood, calling for him. We called all of the houses of his friends that lived nearby. We couldn't find him anywhere so we called the police. When they arrived and Dorito heard-"

"Don't call him *Dorito!*" Reanna admonished.

"When *Doroteo* heard us talking to the police he figured he better come out."

"Why did he hide? What was he so afraid of?"

"I guess he was afraid he was going to get into trouble."

166

"Was he afraid you were going to beat him?"

"No. I don't know," I said. "He was just . . . afraid."

"Have you ever beat Doroteo?"

"No!"

"You've never hit him?"

"I've *spanked* him."

"Really?" she asked. "You hit him?"

"I've *spanked* him."

"I'm not playing semantics with you, Mr. Holland. How many times have you hit Doroteo?"

"I've spanked him twice."

"Exactly twice?" she asked, skeptically. "You remember exactly how many times you've hit him?"

"I remember exactly how many times I've spanked him, yes."

"Why did you hit him the first time?" she asked.

"The first time I spanked him was when we were on a camping trip. He was about five years old. We had a campfire going and he tried to poke a stick into the fire to push the logs around like he'd seen me doing. I told him not to do it. When he did it again I gave him a spanking."

"Made you angry, huh?"

"No," I said. "I didn't want him to get hurt."

"You didn't want him to get hurt, so you hit him?" she asked. "That makes a lot of sense."

I didn't say anything.

"What about the second time?"

"The second time I spanked him was last winter. I'd broken my leg and I was in a cast and it was really hard for me to get around and do stuff. We have a hot tub and Dorito wanted to get in it, but I told him 'No'."

"*Doroteo*," Reanna said through gritted teeth.

"Oh. Right. Doroteo wanted to get in, but I told him 'No', that he'd have to wait until Laci got home-"

"Say, 'His mother'."

167

"What?"

"Instead of calling her 'Laci', call her 'his mother'. We want to take every opportunity we have to remind this judge that Doroteo views you and your wife as his only parents."

"Oh. Okay. So I told *my son, Doroteo*, that he would have to wait until *his mother* got home." Reanna smiled at me and I went on. "I couldn't get into the hot tub with him because of my cast and it was too cold for me to just sit around outside and watch him. Plus, I knew I'd have a hard time getting the cover off by myself."

"And what happened?"

"He went into his room. I thought he was playing, but after a little bit I heard the back door. I hobbled into the kitchen and looked out the window. He was in his bathing suit and he was tugging away at the cover of the hot tub, trying to get it off. I told him it wasn't safe for him to get in the hot tub without an adult there and I gave him a spanking."

"Good," Reanna said in her own voice, nodding approvingly. Then she put her Beckham voice back on and continued. "You're a hunter?"

"How'd you know that?" I asked.

"It's my *job* to know that, David," she said. "Answer the question. Are you a hunter?"

"Yes."

"Have guns in the house?"

"Yes," I said, "but they-"

"Asked and answered," she interrupted. Then, in her own voice she said, "Don't worry – on cross I'll make sure we get it in there that they're locked in a gun safe and they're unloaded and the ammo's locked in a different location and all that . . ."

How did she know all this stuff?

"You and your wife were foster parents for a while, is that true?" Reanna asked.

"Yes." My breath caught in my throat like it always did whenever I thought about Amber.

"Why did you decide to take in a foster child?"

"I . . . I don't know, exactly," I said.

"I want you to answer here, *'Because we found out about a little girl in our son's class that needed a foster family and we wanted to help her out*'," Reanna instructed in her own voice.

"Right," I nodded. "Because my wife and I found out about a little girl who was in Dorito's class that-"

"DOROTEO!"

"Sorry," I said. "Because my wife – I mean – because *his mother* and I found out about a little girl in *Doroteo's* class who needed a foster family and we wanted to help her out."

"But it eventually became necessary to remove that child from your home, correct?"

"Well . . ."

"Yes or no, please."

"Her mother regained custody of her."

"Was she removed from your home or not?" Reanna asked sharply. Then, in a softer voice, she said, "Just say 'Yes' and I'll fix it later."

"Yes," I said reluctantly.

"And in the spring, before she was removed from your home, did you take this little girl with you to California?"

"Yes," I said.

"Did your wife go with you?"

"No."

"Did anyone else go with you?"

"Yes."

"Who?"

"A friend."

"A friend?"

"Yes."

"Who?"

"Tanner Clemmons."

"Tanner," she said, appearing to think. "Is that a male or a female?"

"Male."

She paused.

"Is it true that this little girl came to you from an abusive situation?" she asked me.

"Yes," I said quietly.

"She'd been sexually abused, is that correct?"

"Yes."

"And yet, somehow you thought it was a good idea for her to travel all the way to California with two grown men and no female to accompany her?"

I didn't say anything.

"Answer it," she said, gently. "You've gotta answer it."

"Yes."

She looked at me for a long moment.

"That hardly seems appropriate," she went on in her Beckham voice. "Where did you stay?"

"In a hotel."

"All three of you stayed in the same hotel room?" she asked, incredulous.

"No," I said. "We had two rooms."

"So this little girl was left in a hotel room in a strange city all by herself?"

"No," I said, hesitatingly. "I had a room with two beds in it and she slept in one of them and I slept in the other."

"Uh-huh."

She pretended to shuffle through some papers.

"How soon after you and this *male* friend returned from California with her did Social Services decide to remove her from your home?"

"That's not what happened!" I cried.

"How long, Mr. Holland?" Reanna asked firmly.

"It's not what you think!" I said. "I don't even understand how you

170

know about any of this!"

"It doesn't matter what I think, David," Reanna said gently, putting her hands on the table in front of me and leaning forward. "If I found out about it, I guarantee *they* can find out about it. No matter what they know or what they say or how they twist it, you can't let them see you get angry. Just answer the question honestly and trust that I'm going to come in and clean it up on cross. Okay?"

"Okay," I nodded, "But, seriously. How did you find out about all this stuff?"

"I may have had dinner last night," she said, carefully avoiding my eyes for the first time since I'd met her, "with your male friend – Tanner."

After she'd accused me of being a negligent, gun-toting, child-beating, pedophile, Reanna moved on to some topics that were even more fun, like Greg, Mr. White, and even Gabby. When we were finished, Reanna looked at me approvingly and said that I'd come through with flying colors. I mumbled my thanks to her, went home and took a double dose of ibuprofen. I was lying in my office on my couch/bed, when Tanner called.

"I hate you," I said, answering the phone.

"Tough day?"

"I hate you," I said again, sighing. "What did you tell her about Charlotte?"

"Nothing," he said. "Just that she's like a little sister to you."

"And that she got pregnant last year?"

"Well, yeah . . ."

"Uh-huh. Well, apparently I might be the father of the baby."

"I never said that."

"No, I think Reanna's pretty good at inventing stuff like that all by herself," I agreed. "She also wondered if someone helped me dispose of

171

your father's body or if I did it all by myself."

"She wanted to know everything," Tanner explained. "She said she needed to get you ready in case they started twisting things around when you were on the stand. . ."

"I know," I admitted. "If this Beckham guy had started asking me some of that stuff out of the blue next month I probably would've lost it in front of the judge. I'm ready for anything now, though."

"Good," Tanner said. "I'm glad."

"Me too," I agreed, "but Tanner?"

"What?"

"She'd better not try and bill me for the dinner you ate last night."

~ ~ ~

LACI AND I continued along in our pattern of doing whatever needed to be done while at the same time ignoring each other as much as possible. Laci still cooked the dinner every night and did all the laundry (which was fortunate for me because I didn't really want to start). I guess she figured that since I was paying all the bills, fair was fair. She didn't wash the sheets on my couch/bed though . . . I did that by myself.

At the beginning of December, I took Lily and Dorito out to choose a Christmas tree. After I'd carted it home, put it in the stand, and dragged it into the house, I lugged all of our decorations up from the basement and set them in the living room by the tree. I didn't say one word about it to Laci, but she took over from there, helping the kids string the lights and hang up ornaments.

At least I wasn't obsessing about Amber anymore. As each day passed the hope that I might ever see her again had faded more and more. I no longer fantasized that one day I'd suddenly get a call from her mother, telling me that she'd finally decided to let me see Amber. I knew that was never going to happen and I had given up wishing otherwise. Now I had other things to worry about anyway. Dorito made out his Christmas list and wanted me to help him mail it to Santa. As I let him open the door to the mail slot at the post office, I couldn't help but blink back tears, wondering if this was going to be the last Christmas that I would ever spend with him.

The hearing was scheduled for two weeks before Christmas. Reanna anticipated that the whole thing would take – at the most – two days. Tanner took off three days, just in case (for which I was exceptionally grateful), saying that we could go on a celebratory hunting trip on the third day if the judge had already ruled in our favor by then.

~ ~ ~

OPENING STATEMENTS BEGAN on a Wednesday morning. After Beckham and Reanna had each given the judge a brief rundown of what he could expect, Beckham started things off.

First he presented the results of the DNA tests that showed that Savanna was indeed Dorito's biological mother. Then he submitted marriage, birth, and death certificates to show that Savanna had married her husband, that he was named as Dorito's father, and that he had died over the past summer.

Next Beckham called an expert witness, the psychologist, Zoe Walker. She testified that she had met with Savanna and spoken with her at great lengths. It was Zoe's expert opinion that Savanna had suffered greatly at the hands of her husband, been terrified of him, and had submitted to his wishes and desires in an attempt to not only survive, but to protect her children as best she could. When she began relaying information that Savanna had shared with her, Reanna tried to object, saying it was hearsay, but the judge decided to allow it.

As Dorito became older, Savanna had told Zoe, it became clear that he had needed medical attention for his legs, but the family couldn't afford it. One day, Dorito's biological father took him some distance from their home and abandoned him in a busy park where he knew that Dorito would be quickly found. Savanna's husband came home without the child, refused to tell Savanna where he was, and forbid her from ever searching for him. He also told Savanna that he would kill Dorito if she ever did manage to find him and bring him back into the house. For the next seven years, out of fear for her own safety as well as the safety of Dorito, Savanna never made an attempt to locate her son.

This past summer, Savanna's husband had become gravely ill. He was sick for weeks before he finally passed away and – during that time – he told Savanna exactly where he had left Dorito. Once her husband

174

finally died, Savanna began looking for her son. The orphanage where Laci had worked was the closest one to the park and was naturally the first place that Savanna inquired. The director, Inez, knew immediately which child Savanna was asking about. She told Savanna that Dorito had been adopted, gave Savanna our names, and told her where we lived.

Thanks a lot, Inez.

Reanna cross examined Zoe.

"You work with many women who have been abused by their partners, don't you, Ms. Walker?"

"Yes."

"Have you ever worked with women who have filed restraining orders against their abusive partners?"

"Yes."

"Have you ever worked with a woman who has found relief from their abuse because they filed a restraining order?"

"Yes, but-"

"Have you ever worked with women who went to a safe house because their partner was abusing them?"

"Yes."

"Did any of those women successfully escape their abusive situation by going to a safe house and utilizing the resources that were made available to them there?"

"Yes, but-"

"Have you ever worked with an abused woman who went to the police when her partner beat her?"

"Yes."

"Have any of those abusers subsequently gone to prison as a result of what they did?"

"Yes."

175

"Thank you, Ms. Walker," Reanna said. "I have no further questions at this time."

Beckham then asked Zoe if she also knew of any women who had tried to file a restraining order, go to a safe house, or call the police after being abused who had *not* had such happy outcomes.

She did.

Had any of those women lost their lives because of their attempts to escape abuse?

Yes, they had.

When Beckham was done this time, Reanna didn't ask any more questions.

After Zoe Walker stepped down, Beckham called his next witness.

"Your Honor, we call Claudio Escalante to the stand."

A young, Hispanic man walked forward, swore to tell the whole truth and nothing but the truth, and then took his place on the witness stand. I found myself sitting forward in my seat, my eyes riveted to him.

Dorito's *brother*.

I couldn't help but be fascinated as I saw the same black eyes as Dorito's glancing nervously around the courtroom.

"Please state your name."

"Claudio Escalante."

"And how old are you?"

"Twenty-three."

"Thank you. Mr. Escalante, could you please tell us your relationship to the respondent?"

"Yes," he said with a thick accent. "She ees my mother."

"Your mother?"

"Yes."

"So . . ." Beckham said, as if he were just now piecing this giant

176

mystery together, "that would mean that you are Doroteo's brother?"

"Rogelio."

"I beg your pardon?"

"His name ees Rogelio."

"Oh," Beckham nodded. "I see. Well, right now, in the eyes of this court, his name is Doroteo so we're going to have to refer to him that way, okay?"

"*Sí*. I will try."

"Is Doroteo your brother?"

"*Sí*. Yes."

"Full brother?"

Claudio looked confused.

"Do you have the same mother *and* the same father as Doroteo?"

"Oh," he nodded, understanding. "*Sí* — I mean, yes."

"How many brothers and sisters are in your family?"

"I have two seesters and three brothers."

"Three including Doroteo?"

"Yes."

"Are your other brothers and sisters also older than Doroteo?"

"Yes," he said. "I am the oldest and he is the leetlest."

"And you are all full brothers and sisters?"

"Yes."

"When is the last time you saw Doroteo?"

"Seven and one half years ago."

"What happened on that day?"

"We had breakfast and all go to school except for Rog- Except for Doroteo. He ees too leetle to go."

"How old was he?"

"One and one half years."

"I see. So you went to school that day and when you returned home, tell us what happened."

"When I come home he ees gone."

"Gone?"

"*Sí* . . . yes. Gone."

"Where was he?"

"We do not know," he said, shrugging. "Mama was crying and Papa tell her '*¡Cállate la boca!*'."

"*¡Cállate la boca!?*" Beckham asked.

"How you say? Shut-up."

"Did your mother stop crying?"

"No."

"So what happened then?"

"He heet her."

"Where?"

"Here," Claudio said, making a fist and aiming it at the side of his face. "And here," he touched his nose with his fist. "And here," he jabbed his fist into his ribs.

"And did your mother 'shut-up' after that?"

"A leetle," he said.

"Did you ever see Doroteo again?"

"No."

"But didn't you wonder what happened to him?"

"*Sí*, but Mama tell us not to talk about eet anymore and so we do not ask. We do not want things to be worse."

"Worse?"

"We do not want Papa to heet her anymore."

"Did your father beat your mother frequently?"

"Only if he ees drinking or if he ees mad at her."

"Was she ever injured by him?"

"Oh," he nodded matter-of-factly. "*Sí*. Yes."

"Did she ever go to a hospital because of her injuries?"

"No."

"Why not?"

"No money."

178

"Did she ever receive medical care of any kind for her injuries?" Beckham asked.

"Yes."

"Like what?"

"Our neighbor ees putting bandages on her or putting glass out of her head. She put ice on her. One time she . . . how you say? Give her steetches."

"Did your father ever hit any of the children?"

Claudio looked thoughtful. "No," he finally said. "Not unless we get in the way."

"Get in the way?"

"If he ees heeting her and we ees trying to stop him. Then he would heet us too. We ees not getting in the way very often."

"Claudio, why didn't your mother ever go to the police after your father hurt her?"

"Calls for speculation," Reanna interrupted.

"Claudio," Beckham said, "why didn't *you* ever go to the police and tell them that your father was hurting your mother?"

"He ees her husband," Claudio shrugged.

"Are you married?"

"No."

"If you get married one day, do you think it will be okay for you to beat your wife?"

"I will not be heeting my wife," he said carefully.

"But if you did," Beckham asked, "what would happen to you?"

"No thing," he shrugged.

"Nothing?" Beckham asked, feigning shock. "Are you telling me that you wouldn't be arrested and put in prison?"

"No," Claudio said, shaking his head.

"Are you aware that if a husband were to beat his wife in the United States and was caught, he could go to prison?"

"*Si,*" Claudio shrugged, "but eet ees deeferent in Mexico."

179

"So, is it safe to say that your mother was oppressed by your father?"

"Oppressed?"

"Kept from doing what she wanted to do . . . not free from your father."

"Oh. *Si*. She ees oppressed."

"Why didn't your mother leave your father?"

"Calls for speculation," Reanna interrupted again.

"Did your mother ever talk about leaving your father?" Beckham asked.

"No."

"Do you have an opinion about why that might be?"

"She cannot be leaving him. She ees having seex children. He makes her money and she ees doing what he says. She cannot leave him."

"Thank you, Mr. Escalante. I have no further questions at this time."

Next it was Reanna's turn to question Claudio.

"Mr. Escalante, you testified that your father beat your mother when he was drunk or when he was angry. Is that correct?"

"*Si*. Yes," he nodded.

"And you also testified that to your knowledge, she never sought professional medical treatment for any of the injuries that she sustained during the time she was allegedly abused?"

"No."

"Did you ever take any pictures of any of your mother's injuries?"

"No."

"What is the name of the neighbor who allegedly attended to your mother's various injuries?"

"Her name is Yesenia Jimenez."

"Hmmmm," said Reanna, looking over a piece of paper. "I don't see that name anywhere on the witness list. I guess we'll just have to take your word for that."

"My father hurt my mother," Claudio insisted. "She ees very afraid of him."

"Your Honor!" Reanna implored, looking at Judge Goebeler.

"Mr. Escalante," he said, "please limit your remarks so that you are only answering the questions that Ms. Justice asks of you."

Claudio nodded.

"Mr. Escalante, are you aware that it is against the law in Mexico City for a man to beat his wife?"

"I think eet ees wrong," he nodded.

"No," Reanna said. "I'm not saying that it is just *wrong*. I'm saying that it is against the law in Mexico City. I'm saying that if a man is charged with beating his wife and he is found guilty, he can go to jail. Are you aware of that?"

"I guess," he shrugged.

"Please answer 'Yes' or 'No' Mr. Escalante. Are you aware that it is against the law in Mexico City for a man to beat his wife?"

"Yes."

"And at any point during your parent's marriage, did you ever once report the fact that your father was beating your mother to the authorities."

"No, but I-"

Reanna put up a hand to stop him. "Are you familiar with *Casa de Esperanza* on Las Cruces?"

"No."

"No? Oh. Have you ever heard of *Casa Segura Para Mujeres* on Corrigedora?"

"No."

"Hmmmm. How about *Ministerio de Mujeres En Sus Manos* on Degoltado?"

"No."

"I have a list here of over twenty safe houses for women that are

181

located within Mexico City. I found these after just a brief search – I'm sure there are many more. But is it safe to say that you are not going to have heard of any of them?"

"No," Claudio said, shaking his head. "I have not."

"Mr. Escalante, you *do* live in Mexico City, correct?"

"Yes."

"Since you seem unaware of the existence of any of these safe houses, I assume it would also be safe to say that you never contacted any of them in regard to the fact that your father was abusing your mother?"

"No."

"And I also assume that you never suggested to her that she find a safe place to go where she could get away from your father and be protected from him?"

"No, but-"

"So, let me just clarify here, Mr. Escalante," Reanna interrupted. "To your knowledge – at no point during the course of your parent's marriage did your mother make any attempt to get herself out of an abusive situation. To your knowledge the police were never notified. To your knowledge, she never sought professional help of any kind?"

"No."

"Thank you, Mr. Escalante. I have no further questions at this time."

After Claudio testified the prosecution rested and then it was Reanna's turn.

First she called Dorito's second grade teacher to the witness stand to testify that Laci and I were the most wonderful parents who had ever walked the face of the earth and that Dorito was the most well-adjusted, friendliest and smartest kid she had ever had the pleasure to teach. She also testified how I had volunteered regularly in Dorito's class and how I had not only worked so hard with Amber but had taken her into my home and loved her as one of my own. By the time she had finished, my nomination for sainthood was pretty much in the bag.

After that, Reanna called Amber's social worker, Stacy Reed, to the stand to tell a similar story. The main thing Stacy was able to add was that she could testify to what a safe and nurturing home environment we were providing for our children and how she hoped we would foster another child one day because kids needed parents like me and Laci.

After each woman testified, the judge gave Beckham an opportunity to cross examine them.

"No questions at this time, Your Honor," he said both times.

After Stacy testified, Judge Goebeler decided that we would break for lunch and reconvene in one and a half hours.

"How's it going?" I asked Reanna on the way out.

"About like I expected," she shrugged.

"Is that good or bad?"

She shot me a long look and I shut up.

We walked to a small restaurant not far away from the courthouse.

"Why didn't Beckham ask Dorito's teacher or Stacy any questions?" Tanner wondered as we walked along.

"I don't think he's going to try and show that Doroteo would be better off with Savanna," Reanna said. "I think he knows he doesn't have a snowball's chance of proving that and he's counting on the judge ruling in their favor based strictly on the fact that Savanna never consented to the adoption."

"Is he going to ask me anything?" I asked.

"I doubt it," she said. "I think if he was going to take that route we'd know it by now."

I shot a relieved glance at Tanner.

We arrived at the restaurant and Tanner held the door open for Reanna and me. We found ourselves a table and then Reanna excused herself to go to the restroom, asking us to order her a water, with lemon, when the waitress arrived.

183

"I can't believe that was Dorito's brother," I told Tanner after we were seated, shaking my head.

"Why not?" he asked. "He looks a lot like him."

"I know," I said, "but he's so . . . so old! He's closer to *our* age than he is to Dorito's!"

"I think Dorito's gonna be *short*," Tanner observed.

"Thanks," I said, sarcastically. "I hadn't figured that one out yet."

"Don't worry," Tanner said. "He makes up for it with personality."

I couldn't help but smile.

The waitress arrived and gave us some menus. She took our drink orders and left, just as Reanna was returning to the table. She sat down and then turned to me.

"You're on this afternoon," she said. "You ready?"

"Yeah," I nodded.

"Alright," she said. "Let's go over it one more time – just to make sure."

"But Beckham probably isn't even going to ask me anything!" I protested. "You said so yourself."

"'*Probably*' is the key word there," Reanna said. "I want to make sure you're ready for anything."

"So much for a nice lunch," I muttered, rubbing my eyes with my hands.

When I looked back at Reanna, she was staring at me, unimpressed.

"Hit me with your best shot," I told her. "I'm ready."

By two o'clock I'd been sworn in and found myself sitting in the witness chair. Reanna asked me to state my name, age, what I did for a living, and my relationship to Dorito. I told her that I was his father.

"And your wife is Laci Cline Holland? Is that correct?"

"Yes."

"Is she present in the courtroom today?"

"No."

"Can you tell the court why your wife is not here today?"

"She's home," I said, "with our kids. Doroteo is almost nine years old and he needs her to pick him up after school in just a little bit. Lily is four and she's not in school yet. This hearing – this *situation* – has been very stressful for both of us, but we've worked very hard to make sure the kids don't know that anything is going on. Laci and I felt that it was very important for her to stay home today and keep the kids in their normal routine. We don't want them upset."

"That's very understandable," Reanna nodded. "How did you come to first meet Doroteo?"

"My wife was volunteering at an orphanage in Mexico City. I was working full-time, but I would go to the orphanage in the evenings a lot and help out. I met him there – he was one of the orphans."

"How old was he when you met him?"

"Well, at the time we thought he was about eighteen months old, but now we know that he was almost twenty months old."

Now we also know that his birthday is in November, not January . . .

"So he was walking?"

"No."

"Are you sure? Aren't most babies walking by the time they're twenty months old?"

"He should have been," I agreed, "but he wasn't."

"Why not?"

"He had rickets."

"Rickets?"

"Yes."

"What causes rickets?"

"Your Honor!" Beckham interrupted. "The witness is an engineer, not a medical doctor."

Reanna was ready for him.

185

"Withdrawn," she said, snatching a piece of paper from the table. "According to the National Institute of Health, rickets is a disorder that leads to softening and weakening of the bones and it is caused by a lack of vitamin D, calcium or phosphate."

"Your Honor!" Beckham exclaimed. "Ms. Justice is not a medical doctor either!"

It was obvious that he desperately did not want to allow any evidence that might make Savanna Escalante look as if she hadn't taken good care of Dorito while he'd been with her.

"Your Honor," Reanna stated, "I am simply trying to show that Mr. Holland provided medical care and treatment to the child for a prolonged period of time to establish that he took on the role of caretaker at an early stage in this child's life."

"I'll allow evidence of Mr. Holland's care of the child," the judge decided, "but not of what caused the condition. Continue."

Reanna nodded, knowing she'd gotten it in there anyway.

"How do you know Doroteo had rickets?"

"Once I realized that something was really wrong with his legs, I took him to the doctor."

"You took him to the doctor?"

"Yes."

"Was that normal for volunteers to take the children to the doctor?"

"No."

"So why did you do it?"

"He . . . he needed to see a doctor. Something was wrong."

"So you just took it upon yourself to take him to the doctor?"

"I got permission from the director of the orphanage first."

"I see. And who paid for this?"

"I did."

"Why didn't the orphanage pay for it?"

"Money was tight for them and I knew it was going to take a long time before they ever got around to doing something for him, so I just

186

offered to pay for it so he could get some help quickly."

"Did you do that a lot?"

"Do what a lot?"

"Pay for medical treatment for orphans?"

"No."

"Had you ever paid for one of the children to receive medical treatment before?"

"No."

"Did you ever do it again?"

"No," I said. "Well, I mean, we adopted Lily from the orphanage and we've paid for a lot of things for her, but not while she was still an orphan, no."

"Okay," she said, "so you took him to the doctor even though it was not normal for volunteers to take this upon themselves?"

"Yes."

"And it was at what point that he was diagnosed with rickets?"

"They pretty much diagnosed it right away."

"And what type of medical care was needed?"

"Ummm, well, we had to make sure that he had a more nutritious diet and that he had plenty of vitamin D and got out in the sun . . . that sort of thing."

"Is that all?"

"No," I said. "He needed orthotics and physical therapy."

"Orthotics?"

"Yes," I nodded. "They were these plastic leg braces that helped straighten out his legs."

"I see," Reanna said. "And how long did he have to wear these leg braces?"

"Well, he had three sets total because as he grew they had to make him new ones, and he wore each set for about seven or eight months . . . I guess about two years."

"And physical therapy for two years?"

187

"No," I said, "he got to the point where we just did the exercises ourselves. The physical therapist told me to just to keep him active and encourage him to walk and stuff."

"And did you?"

"Yes," I said.

"How?"

"Ummm, we mostly played. I tried to make it fun for him – you know, instead of saying 'Oh, it's time to do your exercises,' we'd have a contest to see who could reach up the highest – I'd be on my knees and would pretend to reach as high as I could and let him win . . . that sort of thing."

"You were responsible for making sure he went to physical therapy and did his exercises?"

"Yes."

"And was that something that was normal for volunteers at the orphanage to do?"

"No."

"No?"

"No."

"So why did you do it?"

"I wanted to help him. I wanted to make sure he had all the advantages in life that he could."

"And how many times did you take children from the orphanage to physical therapy?"

"I just did it for Doroteo."

"No other orphans?"

"No."

"What about special exercises?"

"No," I said, "just him."

"So," she said, "for no other orphan did you pay for medical care. For no other orphan did you take them to therapy and make sure they did their exercises. Is that correct?"

188

"Yes."

"Why not?" she asked. "Weren't there a lot of other children who probably could have used some extra attention but weren't getting it?"

"Yes," I said.

"But you only helped Doroteo?"

"Yes."

"Why did you want to help him?"

"He . . . he was special to me," I said.

"Special? What made him so special?"

"I don't know," I said, shaking my head. "It's not really something I can explain, but he was just the neatest kid. He still is."

"He's still the neatest kid?" she smiled.

"He's the greatest," I said.

"Tell me something about him," Reanna said. "What's his favorite thing to do?"

"Talk!" I grinned. "He loves to talk!"

I stole a glance at Tanner and saw that he was smiling, too.

"Rather verbose, is he?" she asked.

"You have no idea," I said. "Dorito doesn't even stop talking when he goes under water."

"What did you call him?"

Ooops.

"Ummm, Dorito," I said. I glanced at the judge. "It's his nickname. Everybody calls him that."

"Everybody?" Reanna asked.

"Yes."

"Even his teachers?"

"Yes."

"Who gave him his nickname?"

"Ummm, I did."

"Do you love Dorito?" Reanna asked me quietly.

I nodded, blinking back tears.

"Please answer out loud," she said.

"Yes," I said, my voice breaking.

"How much do you love him?"

"I . . . I can't tell you," I said, shaking my head. "There's no way to quantify how much I love him."

"Try," she urged.

I looked down at my hands and at my wedding ring.

"He's the most important thing in my life," I finally said, looking back up at her. "He's everything to me. I don't know what I would do without him."

~ ~ ~

"THANK YOU," REANNA said gently, and then she looked at the judge. "No further questions."

"Your witness," the judge told Beckham.

"Thank you, Your Honor," Beckham said, "but we have no questions at this time."

I let out a silent sigh of relief and then glanced at the judge.

"You may step down," he said.

"Okay," I nodded. "Thank you."

As I made my way back to my seat, I heard him ask if any other witnesses were going to be called. When he was told that there weren't, it was time for summation.

During closing arguments, Beckham reiterated that Savanna had never abandoned her child, but that Dorito had been kidnapped from her. Furthermore, Beckham stated that Savanna had never had the opportunity to find him or to contest the adoption and termination of her parental rights because her husband had unlawfully prevented her from doing so.

Reanna reminded the judge that our adoption of Dorito had followed all the laws of both countries and that Savanna could have gone to the police any time she wanted to – it wasn't as if she had been locked in a cage in her basement or something. What Dorito's father had done had been illegal and if Savanna had chosen to put up with it and not take any action against him . . . well, that wasn't our problem. The fact of the matter was that Savanna had had a choice as to whether or not to attempt to find her child and she had chosen not to. By choosing not to she had, in effect, abandoned her child just as her husband had.

It was not the place of the court, Reanna went on, to determine *why* a mother would choose to abandon her child – just like it was not the duty of the court to determine *why* a mother might agree to put her child up for adoption. If the courts were allowed to examine the reasons why parents made the decisions that they did, then every unwed, teenaged mother who had ever felt pressured by her parents to get rid of a newborn baby could – years later – change her mind and ask the courts to give her back her child. Once a decision has been made, one must live with the consequences of their decision.

Reanna only hinted at the fact that Savanna had demonstrated an inability to properly care for her children by not attempting to get them out of an abusive situation and by allowing Dorito to get rickets, but she did make a big deal out of what fantastic parents Laci and I were and how happy Dorito was in his home with us – the only parents he had ever known. It would be devastating for him, Reanna wrapped up, to even consider taking him away from us.

That, I decided, was the understatement of the century.

After they were done, I was surprised – and upset – when the judge told us that he was going to wait until the next day to announce his verdict.

"Does he honestly not know how he's going to rule?" I cried to Reanna after court had been adjourned.

"He might not have decided yet," Reanna admitted, "but the fact that he's told us to be back here tomorrow morning makes me think he's already made up his mind. I think he just wants to collect his thoughts and decide how he wants to word his decision."

"What do you think he's going to do?"

She gave me a look that implied I was hopeless.

"I'll see you tomorrow morning," Reanna said, patting me on the shoulder. "Go home and enjoy your evening."

~ ~ ~

WE'D ONLY BEEN on the road for about five minutes when Tanner's phone vibrated. He held it up and looked at it.

"It's Laci," Tanner said, surprised.

I snatched the phone away from him and answered it.

"What are you doing, Laci?" I asked.

"David?"

"Yes! It's David. What are you calling Tanner for?"

"I . . . I wanted to find out how things went today."

"So you called *Tanner?*" I asked.

"Well, *you* won't tell me anything!" she protested.

"Maybe if you'd been there with me like you should have been then you'd *know* what happened."

Laci didn't say anything and Tanner shot me a very disapproving look.

I looked out the window and took a deep breath.

"Are you there?" I finally heard her ask quietly.

"Yes."

"Will you please tell me what happened?"

"The judge isn't going to make a decision until tomorrow."

"Well, how did you feel that things went today?"

"Lousy."

"Why?"

"Because they're focusing on the fact that he was essentially kidnapped. There's no precedent for a kidnapped child *not* being returned to his biological parent after he's been found."

"What do you mean?"

"I mean," I said, trying not to shout, "that we're probably going to lose him, Laci! That's what I mean!"

"But . . . but we adopted him!" she cried. "We legally adopted him

194

and-"

"It doesn't matter, Laci!" I said. "Don't you understand? He was kidnapped! The adoption was never legal because his mother never gave consent for him to be adopted! That's what they're saying!"

"Does your lawyer think we're going to lose him?" she asked.

"She won't tell me what she thinks," I said. "But I can read the writing on the wall. You don't need to have a law degree to see what's going on."

"Is there anything I can do?" she asked.

"It's a little late for that."

"I'm trying to help," she said.

"I've gotta go," I told her.

"Are you coming home?"

"Where else would I go?" I asked, hanging up on her.

"Dave," Tanner said as I thrust his phone at him.

"Don't start, Tanner. Okay? Just *don't start* with me."

He reached for his phone. "You guys can't keep going on like this. You've gotta work it out."

"You're the last person I need marital advice from," I snarled. I saw his hands tighten on the steering wheel and his jaw tense. Of course, shutting-up at this point would have been a good plan, but I was too far gone.

"I don't know what you care for anyway," I said. "Get me out of the picture and you could have her all to yourself."

He actually pulled his truck over to the side of the road. It came to a stop and he turned to face me.

"Do you really think that's what I want?" he asked.

I couldn't bring myself to look at him. No one could ask for a better friend than what he'd been to me over the past year. I was filled with self-loathing.

"No," I finally said. "I don't think that."

Out of the corner of my eye I could see him relax.

"Look," he said quietly. "I saw you do this when Greg died. You took it out on everyone around you . . ."

"I'm sorry," I said. "I'm not mad at you . . . I shouldn't have said that."

"I'm not talking about you taking it out on *me*," he said.

"What are you talking about?"

"Laci," he said.

"I'm taking it out on *Laci* because I'm mad at *Laci*!" I clarified.

"No, you're not," he said.

"Yeah," I argued. "I pretty much am. She's been against me every step of the way – ever since Savanna Escalante darkened our doorstep."

"She's been against the decisions you've made," he agreed, "but that's not why you're mad. Even if Laci had supported you every step of the way, would anything be different right now?"

"Uh, yeah," I said. "I wouldn't be mad at her."

"But wouldn't you still be sitting here waiting for a judge to decide if you get to keep Dorito or not?"

"I guess so," I said.

"And wouldn't Amber still be gone?"

Of course my breath caught in my throat. I didn't answer him.

"And you'd still be mad," he said, shrugging. "And you'd probably still take it out on everybody around you or you'd push everybody away or you'd find some other way to self-destruct. The problem is that you won't let yourself get mad at the right Person."

"The right person?" I asked.

"Yeah. I mean, piss me off ? Well, I might put you in a body cast or something, but you'd probably heal . . . *eventually*. Piss Laci off? She might divorce you or whatever, but probably you'd get over that, too. But piss off the Big Guy upstairs?" he pointed Heavenward and lowered his voice to a dramatic whisper. "I reckon you might be looking at eternal damnation."

"I'm not mad at God," I told him flatly.

196

"And you won't let yourself *admit* that you're mad at God," he went on, "which is probably why you're self-destructing . . ."

"What are you now?" I asked. "A psychotherapist?"

"Nope," he said. "I'm just a big, dumb jock. I probably don't know what I'm talking about at all."

"Are you done?"

"I don't really care if you work things out with God or not," he said, obviously *not* done, "but you need to make things right with Laci. This isn't her fault."

"Can we go home, please?"

"No," he said. "I need you to tell me that you're gonna take care of this before you get back in that courtroom tomorrow."

"I don't think I can," I said quietly, sitting back in my seat and looking out the window.

"You have to," he insisted. "You need to fix things with her *tonight* – before it's too late."

"No. You don't understand," I said. "I think it's already too late."

"*What are you talking about?*"

"I don't think we're gonna be able to work things out."

"That's crazy!" Tanner said. "You guys are having a fight! You don't throw away a whole marriage just because of one little fight!"

"It's not just a fight," I said. "I don't feel the same way about her."

"You still love her," Tanner told me.

I looked out the window and thought for a minute.

"I don't think so," I said. "Not like I used to."

"She still loves you."

"No," I said, shaking my head. "Not really. It's different for her too. I know she loves me, but it's not like it used to be. She loves me like she loves one of the kids or something . . . like she loves some homeless person she sees on the street or like she loves some family that's living at the landfill or like she loves some mother who wants to get her child back. If she had to choose between me and one of them, I don't think she'd pick me."

"She would too."

"What's so funny about it," I went on, ignoring him, "is that the way she is . . . the way she loves other people so much and the way she wants to help everybody? That used to be one of the things about her that I used to love the most, but now . . ."

"Now?"

"Now it's one of the things about her that I hate."

He looked at me for a long moment and finally sat back, defeated.

"You can't just throw everything away without even trying," he said quietly. He sat back up and looked at me. "You could go see a marriage counselor or something. I *know* you guys can work things out!"

"We probably could," I agreed, looking him in the eye. "But-"

"But what?"

"But the thing is," I finally managed to say, "I don't know if I really care."

~ ~ ~

TANNER PULLED BACK out onto the highway. We didn't talk anymore and during the ride home I found myself thinking back to the first year after Greg had died – when I'd gone into a tailspin and everybody had thought that I'd been suicidal. I hadn't actually wanted to die, but I hadn't really wanted to live either. After I'd finally pulled myself out of that, I'd spent the next three years acting like everything was okay and going through the motions everyday – but I still hadn't really been living. I still hadn't let myself actually *feel* anything.

Why?

Until now, I'd always assumed it was because deep down I'd been afraid that if I let myself feel anything it would hurt too much. Better to feel nothing than to feel pain, right? Just like I hadn't let myself cry over Amber until Danica had talked with me and told me that I'd needed to grieve.

But now I wondered. *What if Tanner was right?* What if the thing I'd been afraid to let myself feel wasn't pain, but anger? Was I afraid to let myself be angry at God?

I tried to determine how I was feeling about God right now. How did I feel about the fact that He'd taken Amber from me and that I might lose Dorito? I closed my eyes and asked myself that.

How did I really feel? Was I angry at God?

Yes.

Wow! That thought actually startled me and I opened my eyes.

199

Tanner was absolutely right. Not only was I angry at God, but the thought of being angry at Him scared me to death.

You can't be angry at God! I scolded myself.

But I was.

Like Tanner had said, it was easier to be mad at everybody else around me than to let myself be angry with God.

Being angry at God was dangerous stuff.

I glanced at Tanner. He seemed to have completely given up on me and was concentrating on driving. I rested my head and closed my eyes again and had a long, long talk with God.

~ ~ ~

"LOOK," I SAID before I got out of the car. "I'm sorry."

"Don't apologize to me," he said, staring out the front window.

"I've been thinking about what you said," I ventured. "I think maybe you were right."

"About what?" he asked, still not looking at me.

Everything.

"I'm gonna talk to Laci."

He turned and looked at me.

"Good," he said quietly.

"Thanks for everything . . ."

He nodded.

"Are you still going to come with me tomorrow?" I wanted to know.

"Do you want me to?"

I gave him the slightest of nods.

"Then I'll be here at eight."

"Thanks," I said. He nodded again and I hopped down out of his truck.

I knew I needed to talk to her, but it had been so long since Laci and I had connected that I didn't know what to say . . . how to start. I found myself glancing at her during dinner, trying to remember how I had once felt about her and wondering now about what had happened to us. One time she caught me looking at her and quickly dropped her eyes to her plate, refusing to look up again.

Like always, we let Dorito carry the conversation. Like always, I wordlessly helped Laci load up the dishwasher and put away the leftovers once Lily and Dorito had cleared their places and gone into the living room. Like always, we worked in silence, carefully avoiding each other.

All I had left to do before leaving the kitchen was to throw a stick of butter into the fridge. That's when Laci spoke.

"I love him, too," she said quietly.

I closed the fridge and looked at her. She was standing at the sink with her back to me, her hands on the counter, supporting her weight.

I didn't answer, but I didn't leave either.

"I know you think I don't love him," she finally said, her voice breaking.

"I never said you didn't love him-"

With that she broke down and started crying, gripping the counter. Her head fell forward and her shoulders shook, her breath coming in loud gasps.

I moved toward her. When she felt me touch her, she collapsed onto the sink and started sobbing.

"I don't want to lose him," she cried, "I don't!"

"I know," I whispered, rubbing her back, "I know."

She sobbed harder and we stood there like that in front of the kitchen sink.

After a moment she quieted and seemed to realize that I was still there next to her with my hand on her back. She straightened herself up and turned toward me.

"I don't want to lose you, either," she whispered quietly. She looked at me tearfully and I cupped her face in my hands and wiped her cheeks with my thumbs.

"You're not going to lose me," I promised and she closed her eyes as I pulled her face to mine.

"David . . ." she breathed as I kissed her – her lips, her cheeks, her neck.

When I finally pulled away from her she opened her eyes.

"I'm so sorry," she whispered.

"No," I said, "I'm sorry."

"I should have gone along with you."

"No," I argued, shaking my head. "You were right. If I'd just let her see him in the first place, all this probably wouldn't have happened. It's my fault. I'm sorry."

"Can we play a game?" we heard Dorito ask. He was standing in the entry way between the living room and the kitchen, apparently oblivious to the fact that both of us had been crying.

"What do you want to play?" I asked him.

"Sorry?" he suggested

"How long have you been standing there?"

"I dunno," he shrugged.

I glanced at Laci and we gave each other a little smile.

"Sure," I told Dorito. "Go get it set up and we'll be right there."

"Woohoo!" he cried and we watched him run off into the living room.

We turned back to each other and I tucked a strand of hair behind her ear.

"What happened to us?" she asked softly.

"I don't know," I admitted, winding another lock of her hair around my finger. "I don't have any idea."

I looked into her eyes, wondering how I had ever lost sight of how beautiful she was or of just how much I loved her.

"Come on!" Dorito called from the living room. "It's ready!"

"There's no way that board is set up already," I called back.

"It almost is!"

"Well, finish it!" I yelled before turning to Laci once more. She smiled at me and I cupped her face in my hands again.

"We're going to be alright," I told her.

"Yes," she said, closing her eyes once more as I kissed her again.

"No matter what?" I asked, pulling back and looking at her.

She nodded at me in agreement. "No matter what."

Despite the fact that the next day could potentially signal the beginning of the end, that evening wound up being one of the happiest nights of my life. Laci and I sat as close to each other as we possibly could without being on top of one another and Lily sat on Laci's lap, helping her draw cards. Dorito ran around the board, moving everybody's pieces for them so that we wouldn't have to get up. We laughed and we joked and we hugged. It was like something from a sappy commercial for ice cream or laundry detergent.

At one point Dorito tilted his head and looked at us.

"I like it when we're like this," he said, seriously.

"We do too," Laci said and we grinned at each other again.

Sappy, yes. But also very nice.

~ ~ ~

"I'M GOING TO come with you tomorrow," Laci told me that night, coming out of the bathroom after brushing her teeth. "I want to be there."

"No," I answered, happy that I was going to be sleeping in our bed tonight and not on the couch in my office. "I already gave the judge this big song and dance about how you weren't there because we were trying to make everything as normal for the kids as possible."

"I'm sorry," she whispered miserably, sitting down next to me.

"It's true, though," I said, picking up her hand. "I *do* want things to be normal. I want you to pick Dorito up from school tomorrow and bring him home and have him get started on his homework and stuff – just like you always do."

"Okay," she finally agreed. She leaned forward and kissed me gently.

"What are we going to do?" she whispered, sitting back and looking at me. "What if the judge says we can't keep him?"

"We'll appeal," I told her, reaching up and stroking her hair. "And Reanna says that even if we lose an appeal then they still have to overturn the adoption that we did in Mexico and then we could appeal that and then . . ."

"But what if we never win?"

"Reanna says it could be tied up in the courts for years. If we drag it out long enough he could be a teenager before it's all over. He could tell the judge himself what he wants . . . he's not going to choose to live with her instead of us."

"You didn't tell me that!" she said, dropping my hand in dismay. "You made it sound like he could get taken away from us tomorrow!"

"That's because I was trying to hurt you," I admitted. "I'm sorry."

She looked at me for a minute.

"It's okay," she finally decided, taking my hand again. She thought for a moment. "So, no matter what happens, he'll still be with us for a while?"

"Yes," I said. "Nothing's going to change right away – he's going to be with us for a good, long while."

She nodded and I stroked my thumb across her hand.

"Are you sure you don't want me to come tomorrow?"

"I *want* you there," I clarified, "but, yeah. I'm sure."

"I don't want you to be there alone," she protested. "Is Tanner going to go with you?"

"Yeah."

"Okay, good," she sighed. "I'm glad he's going."

"I am, too," I said.

That night Laci and I prayed together for the first time in over eight weeks. It was actually the first time in three months that I'd prayed at all except for my desperate pleas of *Please don't take Dorito from me* and the one single prayer I'd offered up to God in Tanner's truck that afternoon. And after we'd prayed, Laci and I talked and kissed and cried and made up – long into the night.

~ ~ ~

LATER, LACI FELL asleep with her head on my shoulder. I was on my back with one arm under my head and another wrapped around her, staring up at the dark ceiling and thinking about something that had been bothering me ever since Tanner and I had talked. Something Tanner had said.

I don't really care if you work things out with God or not.

I knew Tanner believed in God (he talked about Him from time to time, but it was usually with very little reverence). But reverent or not, even if Tanner believed in God, that was a far cry from loving God. And loving God was great, but it wasn't the same as accepting the fact that Christ had died on the cross for your sins.

Simply put, I was pretty sure that Tanner wasn't saved.

Trying to share anything about Christ with Tanner had always been a challenge for me. It was weird how I could talk to strangers about what Jesus had done on the cross all day long, but give me someone I really cared about? Whole other story.

I don't know why it was so hard for me to talk about it with Tanner, but it was. Plus, he didn't want to hear it. Anytime I tried to talk to him about it, he always changed the subject or told me to shut up. Maybe that's why it was so hard . . .

Laci stirred in her sleep and started to turn away from me, but I tightened my arm around her to keep her against me. This was enough to wake her up and she lifted her head off of my shoulder and looked at me in the dim light.

"Hi," she said, and I could tell from the way her voice sounded that she was smiling.

"Hi," I answered back.

"I'm not dreaming, am I?" she asked.

"No," I smiled back, squeezing her.

207

"What are you doing?" she asked.

"Thinkin' about stuff."

"What kind of stuff?"

"Tanner."

She propped up on one elbow. "*Really?*" she exclaimed. "I'm laying here like this next to you for the first time in *months* – and you're thinking about *Tanner?*"

"Sorry," I said sheepishly.

"You're worried about him," she stated quietly. (We'd had this conversation before.)

I nodded.

She put her head back on my shoulder and rested her hand on my chest and I thought of everything that Tanner had done for me over the past year. Honestly, I didn't know how I could have gotten through it all without him.

And what had I done for him in return?

Nothing.

I couldn't even bring myself to have a conversation with him about what I knew was the most important thing in the world.

Some friend I was . . .

"Laci?"

"Hmmm?"

"Can I ask you something?"

"Sure," she said, propping back up on her elbow.

"When you and Tanner were dating," I began, "did you two ever talk about . . . about God?"

"When we *broke up* we talked about Him," she said wryly.

"So he knows?"

"Knows what?"

"Knows that the reason you two broke up is because it was God's will for you and me to be together?"

"Yeah," she said with a derisive laugh. "He knows."

"You didn't talk about God with him any other time while you were going out?"

"No," she said quietly.

"Really? I can't believe that."

"Why's it so hard to believe?" she asked. "You know how hard he is to talk to about stuff like that."

"No, I know that, but what I can't believe is that *you* – of all people – would go out with someone that you couldn't talk to about God with! God's the most important thing in your life!"

"I already told you," she said. "I'd gotten pretty far away from God at that point in my life. Being able to talk with someone about God wasn't exactly what I was looking for in a boyfriend."

"What were you looking for?"

"Oh, no," she worried. "You're not gonna start obsessing about *this* now, are you?"

"No," I promised. "But, that is something I've never really been able to figure out. If you were going to date someone . . . why *Tanner?*"

She looked at me in the darkness and finally sighed, laying back on her pillow and staring up at the ceiling. I rolled over on my side and faced her, waiting.

"Because I loved him," she finally said, reluctantly.

"I know you loved him," I answered. "I'm asking *why?* Why did you love Tanner?"

She sighed again and thought for another moment.

"You know what he's like" she began. "He's a lot of fun, he's nice. We had a good time doing things together . . ."

I didn't ask her what *things* she was talking about.

"He was always there for me . . . he would do anything for me," she went on. "And I guess . . . I guess I loved him because – because he loved me so much."

"Do you really think he loved you?" I asked her.

"I *know* he loved me," she said with certainty.

"That's what you said last time I asked you that."

"Then why do you keep asking me?" she wondered, sounding offended. "Why can't you believe that he really loved me?"

"I believe," I said, propping myself up on one elbow and stroking her cheek with my finger, "that you are the most beautiful woman to ever walk the face of this planet."

She smiled at me in the dim light.

"And," I continued, "I find it *easy* to believe that Tanner or any other man could fall in love with you, but . . ."

"But what?"

"But something just doesn't make sense to me."

"Like what?"

"Like you said that he'd never told anybody else before you that he loved them."

"Right . . ."

"And I can't think of anyone he's dated *since* then that he might have loved, can you? I mean he *lived* with Megan and I know for a fact that he didn't love her."

"So?"

"So, if he really did love you, Laci," I said, "then you're the only woman he's ever loved."

She didn't say anything.

"And . . . and if you're the only woman that he's ever loved, and I'm the reason the two of you aren't together anymore . . ."

She remained quiet.

"Then why is he my friend?"

She still didn't answer.

"I mean . . . by all rights, Laci," I said, "he should hate me! He shouldn't be able to stand being around me . . . around *us!* Why doesn't it bother him that you and I are together?"

"Because he got over me," she said simply. "He doesn't love me anymore."

210

"You really think that?"

"Yes," she said. "We broke up and Tanner got over it. He moved on. I don't think about him that way anymore and he doesn't think about me that way anymore."

"Maybe you're right," I said.

"I know I'm right. Now," she said, reaching her hand up to the back of my neck, "do you really want to lay here and talk about Tanner all night or are there some other things that we could be doing right now?"

"I guess there are some other things we could be doing," I admitted and I let her draw my lips to hers.

But even as she was kissing me, I kept thinking about the fact that Tanner was my friend. And I couldn't help but wonder why.

What exactly, I asked myself, *was in it for him?*

~ ~ ~

DESPITE THE FACT that Dorito was "*going to be with us for a good, long while*", I gave him an extra-long hug in the morning when I dropped him off at school.

"I love you, buddy," I said as someone in a blaze orange vest opened his car door.

"I love you, too," he said, scrambling out. The blaze orange vest slammed his door shut and I watched after him, hoping he'd remember to turn and wave at me.

He did.

I waved back and flashed him the *I Love You* sign. He did it back, following it up with the peace sign, because that meant, *I Love You, Too.*

I stayed and watched until he had disappeared through the giant metal doors, not caring if there was a line of parents behind me, anxious to drop their kids off and get their day started.

I love you, Dorito, I thought. *No matter what happens – I hope you will always know how much I love you.*

At home I found that Laci had made me my favorite breakfast – hash brown potatoes and sausage.

"Thank you," I said, hugging her. "It smells great."

"Sit down," she said, rubbing a hand over my shoulders. "I'll pour you some juice."

I sat down, looked at my plate, and then back up at her.

"What?" she asked.

"If I eat anything I'm gonna get sick," I confessed.

She looked at me sympathetically.

"Don't worry about it," she said, taking my plate away.

"I *really* appreciate it," I told her.

"I know you do," she said, setting my plate on the counter and coming back to me. I pulled her onto my lap and wrapped my arms

212

around her. She hugged me back and put her cheek on the top of my head. After a moment we heard Lily talking to her stuffed animals in her bedroom.

"Sounds like somebody's up," I said.

"I'll go get her," Laci offered.

"No," I said. "I'll go get her. You sit down and eat."

"I'm not going to be able to eat either."

"Well," I said. "Wrap it up and we'll have it for dinner. I'll go get Lily."

"Okay," she agreed, and I went to get our daughter.

Tanner was late, but just when I worried that he wasn't coming he pulled up in the drive. Laci followed me to the door. I opened it up and held up one finger to Tanner to let him know that I'd be right there.

"Are you sure you don't want me to go with you?" Laci asked, wrapping her arms around me.

I found myself wishing that she was, but she was still in her bathrobe and Tanner and I needed to get going. Plus, I really had meant what I'd said earlier about her picking Dorito up from school like she always did.

"I'm sure," I said, pulling her close. "I'll call you as soon as I know something."

"Okay," she nodded, giving me one last, long kiss.

"Bye."

"Bye."

"I love you."

"I love you, too."

I squeezed her and then jogged to the driveway where Tanner was waiting in his truck.

"You're late," I pointed out.

"I'll drive extra fast to make up for it."

"No," I said, hastily doing up my seat belt. "That's okay."

"I wonder how much marriage counselors make?" he mused. I suppressed a smile.

"So suddenly you and Laci are alright?" he asked after a moment.

"Not suddenly," I said, "but we're alright."

"You're welcome," he said.

"Thank you," I acknowledged.

He turned left at the end of our block and picked up speed. I sat quietly for a moment, thinking about the conversation I'd had last night with Laci.

"Why are we friends?" I asked Tanner, breaking the silence.

"I beg your pardon?"

"How come you and I are friends?"

"I dunno," he shrugged. "We have a lot in common."

"Like what?"

"Gee," he said sarcastically, "let's think about this for a minute. What's something we do together?"

"I know we both like shooting and fishing and stuff," I said, "but so do a million other guys. What makes us special?"

"What makes us *special?*" he asked, glancing at me apprehensively. "Please tell me you didn't just say that."

I smirked at him.

"I think you need to go back to San Francisco," he told me.

"Come on," I said. "I'm serious. Why are we friends?"

"We've been friends since we were three years old, and now all of a sudden you want to know *why?*"

"Uh-huh."

"Why?"

"I dunno," I said. "I guess because yesterday you started acting like a psychiatrist and now you've got me thinking about stuff."

"And so now we've gotta have a mushy conversation about why we're friends?"

214

"You started it," I pointed out.

"Yeah," he agreed, "but only because I wanted you and Laci to get back together. That mission's accomplished, so the conversation's over."

"But why do you care so much if things are okay between me and Laci? What's it to you?"

"Because I want you guys to be happy," he said.

"Why?"

"Because we're friends."

"Exactly," I said. "So why are we friends?"

"Oh, brother," he shook his head.

"Maybe you hang around with me just so you can see Laci from time to time," I said with a laugh in my voice so he'd know that (for the most part) I wasn't serious.

"Yes," he said sarcastically. "I'm still so in love with Laci that I'm willing to spend twenty hours a week pretending I give a rat's behind about you in hopes of catching a glimpse of her in her bathrobe every now and then."

"'*Still so in love*'?" I asked. "Does that mean that you're admitting you really *were* in love with her?"

I may have imagined it, but – for the briefest instant – Tanner actually seemed somewhat unnerved.

"If you really want to know," he said, recovering quickly and reaching over to pat my hand, "It's not *Laci* that I've been in love with all these years . . ."

"Yes," I agreed, pulling my hand away from his. "The endless parade of ladies through your bedroom is just a facade until I come to my senses."

"Why are we having this conversation?"

"It's keeping my mind off the trial."

"I see."

"So seriously, why are you my friend?"

"I don't know, David," he said, beginning to sound exasperated.

"Why are you *my* friend? I mean, actually, I'm quite surprised that you're willing to hang around with someone who used to sleep with your wife!"

"WOW!" I exclaimed. "You are *really* desperate to change the subject here, aren't you?"

"It doesn't bother you that I slept with you wife?"

"She wasn't my wife at the time," I smiled. "And you didn't sleep with her."

"I could have," he insisted.

"Yes," I said. "I know. No woman can resist the great *Tanner Clemmons' Charm*. Thank you so much for not turning it on when you were dating Laci."

"You're welcome."

"So come on," I said. "Tell me why you're my friend."

"You go first," he said. "You tell me why you're my friend and then I'll come up with something."

"I dunno," I shrugged.

"See!" he said triumphantly. "You can't tell me why you're friends with me, either!"

"Well, actually, yeah, I can," I said. "Laci and I talked about this last night."

"Talked about what last night?"

"Why we like you."

"Really?" he asked, sounding rather pleased. "You actually had a *'Things We Like About Tanner'* conversation?"

"Yes," I nodded. "It was the happiest moment of my life."

"I can't wait to hear this! Tell me. Start with why Laci likes me."

"Actually," I said, "we both like you for pretty much the same reasons."

"My tush?"

"Uhhh, no. That wasn't on my list."

"Was it on Laci's list?"

"I have no idea. Surprisingly, I didn't ask her how she felt about your tush."

"Find out, will you?" he asked. "Report back to me."

"Uh-huh," I said. "I'll ask her right after I tell her whether or not we get to keep Dorito."

"Thanks."

"Uh-huh."

"So tell me," he said. "I wanna hear the list."

"There wasn't a list."

"You said my tush wasn't at the top of the list, so there must have been a list."

"Well . . . it's a very short list."

"Hit me," he said.

"Okay," I said, smiling. "You're a lot of fun to be around."

"That's a given," he said. "Tell me something I don't already know."

"That's all I can remember," I said. "I told you it was a short list."

He gave me a sideways glance.

"Okay," I went on. "You're very dependable."

"Like a Labrador retriever?"

"No," I laughed. "Like we can count on you. You're always there, always willing to do whatever you can to help us."

"So I'm fun and I'm helpful. That's great."

"Not just helpful," I said. "You would do anything for us. *Anything*. It says in the Bible, that no one shows a greater love than when he lays his life down for his friends."

I ventured a glance at him and saw that he was getting edgy, fast. I moved on quickly.

"That's how you are," I explained. "I know that you'd give your life for me. Or for Laci. Or for my kids. I know that I can count on you for anything."

"Yes," he said, keeping his eyes on the road. "I'm a saint."

"So, that's basically why I'm friends with you," I said. "Now it's your turn. Why are you my friend?"

"I don't know."

"Oh, come on!" I cried. "I said all this nice stuff about you and you can't come up with one single thing to tell me?"

"You've got nice hair."

I sighed.

"And you're really fun to pick on."

I glared at him.

"There," he said. "That's *two* things."

"I tell ya, Tanner. I'm really feelin' the love."

"I don't know!" he said, sounding exasperated again. "I don't know *why* I'm friends with you! We get along! I enjoy being around you! Isn't that enough?"

"I guess," I said, reluctantly.

We rode quietly for a few minutes.

"You know," I ventured after a few minutes, "I've been thinking about something else you said yesterday . . ."

"Don't," he said.

"Don't what?"

"Don't start proselytizing."

"I wasn't going to start proselytizing!" I protested.

"Uh-huh."

I thought for a moment and then asked, "How exactly do you define proselytizing?"

"Talking to me in any way, shape or form about God."

I sighed heavily.

"Amazed that I know you so well?" he asked, glancing my way.

"You're exceptionally insightful for a big, dumb jock," I admitted.

He gave me a self-satisfied smile as we drove on.

"It wouldn't hurt you to talk about God," I said after a moment, breaking the silence.

"No," he agreed, "but that doesn't mean I'm gonna."

I looked at him.

218

"It really bothers me that you won't talk to me about this."

He glanced at me and then put his eyes back on the road.

"Look," he said rather reluctantly after a minute. "If it makes you feel any better, I'm reading the Bible every day."

"*Really?*" I asked, trying not to sound too excited.

"Yeah."

"Well . . . well that's great!"

"Uh-huh."

"Any particular reason?"

"Just because," he said curtly. "I'm just doing it, okay?"

"Okay," I nodded. I tried to drop it, but I couldn't keep myself from asking, "What are you reading right now?"

"Acts."

"Ooooh," I said. "That's one of my favorites."

He rolled his eyes at me.

"I'm not an expert or anything," I offered tentatively, "but if you ever have any questions or anything . . ."

"No," he assured me quickly. "I've got it covered."

"Okay," I agreed, deciding to stop pushing my luck.

"But," he went on, "if I suddenly decide to go get dunked in a river or something, I'll let you know."

"You promise?"

"Yeah," he nodded. "I promise. As a matter of fact – if I decide to do it – you can be the one to push me under."

~ ~ ~

WE BARELY MADE it into the courtroom before the bailiff called our case and Judge Goebeler announced his decision.

"The complexities of this case," he began, reading from a paper that he held in his hand, "have forced this court to consider not only what is in the best interest of the child, but also to examine the legal rights of both the petitioner and the respondent. If the court were to only consider the well-being of the child, it would undoubtedly be forced to rule in favor of the petitioner. The child has known no other family for the past five years and has been, by all accounts, incredibly nurtured and happy in that environment. To disrupt such familiarity and success at this stage would, no doubt, be traumatic – to say the least.

"However," (why did he have to go and ruin his little speech with the word *however?*), "in a case where a child has been clearly kidnapped from his or her parent, the return of that child to the parent upon their recovery is almost always guaranteed, regardless of the happiness and emotional stability of that child in their new situation.

"The court finds that the determining factors in this case come down to whether or not the child was indeed kidnapped from the respondent, and whether or not the respondent was given the opportunity to contest the termination of her parental rights and the subsequent adoption petition."

This, I thought frantically, *is exactly what Beckham has been banking on.*

"The act of kidnapping," the judge went on, "is defined as the crime of unlawfully seizing and carrying away a person by force. The respondent has presented compelling evidence to support the claim that the child was indeed taken from her unlawfully and by force. Furthermore, the respondent has submitted evidence that she was unlawfully prevented from locating the child and from contesting the termination of her parental rights and the subsequent adoption. It is the belief of this court

220

that the respondent did not intentionally abandon her child, nor was it ever her desire to relinquish her parental rights."

I glanced at Reanna, hoping that something in her body language would signal me that she wasn't worried too, but she just stared tensely at the judge.

"However," (suddenly I *loved* that word), "the court has further examined the actions of the respondent following the kidnapping and has found no evidence that any attempt was made by the respondent to find the child. Many legal avenues were available to the respondent, but none of those options were pursued. No police reports were filed. No searches were made of the local orphanages. No media were alerted to the fact that the child was missing. By failing to take any action to attempt to regain custody of the child, the respondent was, in effect, consenting to the actions of her husband."

I noticed Reanna's head give a slight but encouraging nod. I looked back at the judge.

"I would like to take this opportunity to make it clear that the court believes that the respondent was indeed under duress and that her failure to take action to recover the child was due to the fact that she was in an abusive situation and feared for the safety of both herself and her children. Nevertheless, other options *were* available to her and by not pursuing them she was, in essence, condoning the actions of her husband and abandoning her child. The court finds that once the child was abandoned, he was then legally considered an orphan and thereby eligible for his subsequent adoption."

For the first time, Judge Goebeler glanced up from his papers and looked directly at Savanna.

"Mrs. Escalante, this court feels your loss. You have endured much hardship and my sympathies lie with you. However, as Ms. Justice stated in her closing arguments, this court cannot be placed in a position of considering *why* you made the decision you made. The fact of the matter is that you – for whatever reason – made a decision to abandon your child.

Once that decision was made, your son was legally an orphan and was subsequently eligible for adoption."

He returned his gaze to the papers.

"I find that legally the respondent has no claim to her biological son. Furthermore, I find that all actions taken by the petitioners and by all parties involved in both the international and state adoptions are found to be in full compliance with the laws of both countries and with this state.

"Therefore, the respondent's counterclaims to set aside the adoption and the petition for termination of parental rights are denied. Furthermore, it is the ruling of this court that full and legal custody of the minor child shall remain with his adoptive parents, David and Laci Holland. Case dismissed."

Reanna slapped her hand on the table and whipped around to face me. The judge looked at the bailiff.

"We'll reconvene in ten minutes," he said, rising from his seat. The bailiff nodded and called a recess.

Everything was kind of a blur after that. Reanna reached back, put her arm around my shoulder, and gave me a little squeeze. She and Tanner squeezed each other too, and then Tanner gripped me in a giant bear hug and lifted me right up off of the floor.

"We did it!" Tanner yelled, practically squeezing every molecule of air from my lungs. "We did it!"

I nodded at him dumbly with my mouth open as he put me back down, unable to think of anything to say.

"Congratulations," Reanna said to me.

I nodded at her, too.

It was over . . . DORITO WAS MINE!

It was with that realization that I slowly turned to look at Savanna Escalante – Dorito's mother. She had her face buried in her hands, her eyes covered. She sat like that for a long moment, her lips moving silently.

Wasn't that exactly what I must have looked like when the judge had ruled that Karen would get Amber back? What words had I been mouthing silently to God when I'd lost Amber?

No, God – don't take her from me! Don't let this happen! Please don't take Amber from me!

"Cheer up!" Tanner cried, pounding me on the shoulder. I turned to look at him – his grin was stretching from ear to ear. "You won! Didn't you hear what the judge just said? You WON!"

"I heard," I said softly.

"What's wrong?"

I answered him by looking back at Savanna. Her hands were on the table now and she had opened her eyes. Her lawyer was talking to her quietly with one hand on her shoulder. She was listening to him and nodding, tears streaming down her cheeks.

I looked back at Tanner. He glanced at Savanna and then back to me.

"She's *fine*," Tanner said hastily, sternly shaking my shoulder. "She'll be *fine*."

"Like I'm fine without Amber?" I asked.

"This is totally different," he said, shaking his head

"How? How is it different?"

We stared at each other for a long moment.

"Don't do this," he said quietly. "*Don't.*"

I kept looking at him.

"Come on!" he urged, his hand tugging on my shoulder. "We've gotta go. We've gotta call Laci!"

"No," I said, shaking my head and looking back to Savanna. "I have to go talk to her."

"Why?"

I looked back at him and didn't say anything.

"What are you going to do?"

"You know what I'm going to do," I answered quietly, looking straight into his eyes. His hand was still on my shoulder.

"Don't." He shook his head. "Don't."

"I have to."

"No, you don't," he said, distraught.

"Yes, I do."

He looked at me for a minute, but then finally relented and took his hand off of my shoulder.

I looked at my best friend for a long, long moment.

"It'll be okay," I promised. "Everything'll be okay."

And then I went to tell Savanna Escalante that my family was moving back to Mexico.

~ ~ ~

Thank you for continuing to follow David on his journey. I hope you've enjoyed reading *The Other Mothers* and that you'll join David one more time for *Gone*. *Gone* is the final book to be told by David, but it is not the last book in the *Chop, Chop* series. After *Gone*, look for *Not Quickly Broken* (which is told by Jordan and gives you a glimpse into the first few years of his life with Charlotte and *Alone* (told by Tanner and tentatively scheduled to be the last book in the *Chop, Chop* series).

In the meantime, here are the first few pages of *Gone*. The story begins more than twenty years after Laci and David have returned to Mexico . . . enjoy!

L.N. Cronk

Gone
Book Six

Someone was laying on their horn and – for some reason – I was shaking. Looking ahead, I saw a driveway and I pulled in.

I turned the car off, rubbed my forehead, and sat there until I'd calmed down. Then I sighed and looked around.

Where *was* I?

A woman came out of the house and walked toward the car, staring at me suspiciously.

I rolled down my window.

"*Hola*," I said, trying to look as friendly as possible.

She nodded.

"*Me puedes decir como llegar a . . .*"

Can you tell me how to get to . . .

I wasn't really sure what to ask her because I was so lost. I finally decided I'd better just get to Zocaló in the heart of Mexico City because I could get *anywhere* from there.

"*¿Plaza de la Constitución el Zocaló?*" I finally asked.

She looked at me strangely and finally pointed.

"*Ve por ese camino . . . vira a la derecha a la Carretera Federal Ochenta y Cinco. Mantenga en esa dirección algunos treinta minutos y debería ver unos señales de tránsito.*"

Go that way . . . turn right onto highway eighty-five. Stay on that for about thirty minutes and you should see some signs.

Thirty minutes?

I *lived* thirty minutes from Zocaló. And I was going to have another thirty minutes to go on top of that?

I thanked her, pulled away and sighed again, hoping I'd recognize something along the way.

I didn't.

Half of an hour later I finally saw the Metropolitan Cathedral and was surprised at the rush of relief I felt. I turned right onto Medero and drove for a while.

Beginning to relax, I realized how hungry I was. I pulled in to the same McDonald's where I'd bought a thousand Happy Meals. I ordered a double cheeseburger, large fries and a drink and started home.

When I finally arrived I was surprised to find the door open. Laci was usually pretty good about locking up before she left.

Oh well.

I crammed my McDonald's bag into the trash, headed down the hall to my office, and got to work.

By dinnertime Laci wasn't home so I called her.

"I'm working late tonight, remember?"

226

"You are?"

"Yes . . . we talked about it this morning."

"Oh," I said. "I guess I forgot. What am I supposed to do for dinner?"

"I told you I left some meatloaf and potatoes on a plate in the fridge for you to heat up."

I opened the fridge and looked around.

"There's nothing here," I told her.

There was a long pause.

"Are you sure?"

"Of course, I'm sure."

"Did you eat it for lunch?"

"No," I said. "I went to McDonald's for lunch."

There was another long pause.

"I'm gonna come home," she said.

"No, Laci," I said. "It's no big deal. I'll find something to eat."

"No," she said. "I'll pick up something and bring it home."

"That's ridiculous, Laci," I said. "I don't need you to come home. You stay there and get done whatever you need to get done. I'll find myself something to eat."

"Are you sure?"

"Sure, I'm sure," I said. "I'm perfectly capable of taking care of myself."

The next night the table was set for three.

"We're having company?" I asked.

"Dorito's coming for dinner."

Dorito's real name was Doroteo. He was the only one of our children who still lived near us.

"Just Dorito?" I asked, disappointed that his wife and kids weren't coming.

"Ayla has a soccer game," she explained.

"And Dorito's not going to it?" I asked.

"He's coming for dinner," she said again.

Obviously.

He came in the door just as Laci was dishing up and hugged me.

"Hi, Dad," he said as I pounded him on the back.

"How you doing?" I asked.

"Fine," he said, turning to Laci. He gave her what seemed like an extra-long hug.

During dinner I tried to ask him about the kids and about work, but he was very quiet (not a word usually used to describe Dorito).

"So, how come you aren't at Ayla's game?" I finally asked.

"I just . . . I just wanted to see you guys," he shrugged, looking down at his plate.

"Dorito," I finally asked. "Is everything okay?"

"Sure, Dad," he nodded, not looking up from his plate.

I put down my fork.

"Obviously it's not," I said. "What's wrong?"

I saw him take a breath and then look up at Laci for help. That's when I realized she was already in on this.

"Would somebody care to tell me what's going on?" I asked.

Dorito pushed his chair away from the table. He went to the freezer and got some ice for his glass.

I looked at Laci expectantly.

"We just wanted to talk to you about something," she finally said. "But I thought we'd wait until after dinner."

"Well, you might as well just talk to me about it now," I said.

Laci looked up at Dorito. Dorito looked back at her and then set his glass down.

228

"Are the kids okay?" I asked, unable to keep panic from sneaking into my voice. "Is somebody sick?"

"No, no," Dorito assured me, sitting back down and putting a hand on my shoulder. "Everybody's fine."

"So what's this all about then?"

"David," Laci said gently, looking at me and putting her hand on mine. "We're just . . . we've just been a bit worried about you, that's all."

"About *me*?"

I laughed as my panic quickly subsided. "Why would you be worried about me?"

"You seem a little . . . distracted lately," she said carefully.

"What do you mean?"

"I mean . . . like you're not paying attention to things the way you used to."

"I've guess my mind's just been on the addition," I told her.

The orphanage where Laci worked (and where half of our children had come from) had just received the funding they needed to add a huge new wing. The firm I worked for was in charge of the project and I was the lead engineer.

"I've just been thinking about it a lot lately," I assured her. "I'm excited about it!"

"No," Laci said, shaking her head. "This has been going on longer than that."

"What are you talking about?"

"I mean . . . I mean, you're doing things that aren't . . . right."

"Things that aren't *right*?"

"Not . . . normal," she said hesitantly.

"Normal . . ."

She nodded.

"Such as?"

She quickly glanced at Dorito before she went on.

"I tell you things, David, and then later you don't even remember that we talked."

"Everybody does that sometimes."

"Yes," she agreed, "*sometimes* . . . but you're doing it a lot more than just sometimes."

"You're making a big deal out of nothing," I said, waving my hand at her dismissively.

"That's not all," Laci said.

"What?"

"Do you remember a couple of weeks ago when I came home and you were out in the driveway in the car?"

"Yes," I lied.

"Well, you were just *sitting* there!" she said. "And I think you'd *been* sitting there for a long time."

"No I hadn't," I told her. "I was just thinking about something! I've had a lot on my mind."

She sighed and I looked at Dorito.

"I've been fine, haven't I?" I asked him.

"You haven't . . . you haven't been yourself lately," he answered.

"Oh, brother," I said, rolling my eyes. "This is ridiculous. I can't believe she's got you convinced that something's wrong too."

"We want you to go see a doctor," Laci said. "Just go have a check-up, make sure everything's okay."

"So you think I'm crazy?"

"No!" Laci insisted. "I don't think you're crazy at all! I think – I just think maybe something's stressing you out or something and that we should talk to a doctor about it."

"Right now," I said, "*you're* stressing me out."

"Look," Dorito said. "Why don't you just go see a doctor and make Mom feel better?"

"Fine," I agreed. "When we go home next summer I'll tell Dr. Keener that you're worried."

I didn't go to a doctor in Mexico unless I really had to. We went back to the States often enough that I could schedule any annual check-up type stuff when we were home.

"Mike doesn't think this needs to wait eight months," she said.

"You called *Mike* about this?" I yelled. Mike was one of my best friends. He also happened to be a physician.

"I just wanted to-"

"You had *NO* right to do that Laci!" I shouted, slamming my hand down on the table. Laci jumped. "There's nothing wrong with me!"

"Dad-"

"You stay out of this!" I yelled.

"Dad," Dorito persisted, "I came over here last month to trim for you and you'd filled the weed eater up with milk."

"I did not!"

"*Yes*, you did. There was a jug of rancid milk sitting right next to it."

"Who asked you for your help anyway?" I snapped at him. "I can take care of my own yard – you leave my weed eater alone!"

"Your weed eater is *ruined*," Dorito mumbled under his breath.

"Well, I didn't do it!" I cried. "*Somebody* might have done it, but it wasn't me!"

"Who would have touched your weed eater?" Laci asked.

"Maybe you did it," I accused her.

"Why would I do that?"

I decided I'd better back off before they accused me of being paranoid, too.

"I don't know, Laci. What I'm saying is, why would *I* have done it?"

"Grace told me she called you Monday," Dorito said. "She said . . . she said you acted like you didn't even know who she was!"

"You think I don't know my own kids?" I cried. I started ticking them off on my fingers. "There's *Grace* and *Marco* and *Meredith* and *Lily* and *Amber-*"

"David," Laci interrupted, worriedly, "Monday you went to the store to get some bread and you were gone for *five* hours! You wouldn't answer your phone and when you finally came home you didn't have any bread."

I had absolutely no idea what she was talking about.

"So, because my phone wasn't working right and I forgot some bread you're ready to lock me up?"

"No one said anything about locking you up! All we want is for you to go to the doctor to see if they can figure out what's going on."

"Nothing's going on! I'm fine and I don't need a doctor to tell me that I'm fine!"

"What's it gonna hurt to go see a doctor?" Dorito asked. "If you're so sure you're fine, then why don't you just humor us and go to the doctor?"

"No," I said, standing up. "If you're still worried about it next summer then I'll talk to Dr. Keener, but I don't want to hear another word about it until then. Do you understand?" ,

"But-" Laci started.

"Not another word!"

"Please sit down, David," she pleaded. "I won't talk about it anymore. Sit down and finish your dinner."

"I've lost my appetite," I told her and I stalked away.

At two in the morning I got out of bed.

"Where're you going?" Laci asked.

"I'm going to go get that *bread* that you wanted," I muttered under my breath.

"What?"

"I'm getting some cough medicine, Laci."

"You haven't been coughing."

"Yes, I have. I don't feel good."

I rifled around in the medicine cabinet until I found a bottle that was left over from when one of us had had bronchitis or something.

Do not take except under the supervision of a physician. Do not operate a motor vehicle or heavy machinery when taking this medicine.
Warning: *This medication causes drowsiness.*

That sounded good.

I measured out the recommended dosage, tossed my head back and gulped it down.

The next day I was in my office going over the survey of the property for the new wing. I opened my bottom desk drawer to get a file and found a bunch of forks, knives and spoons. I stared at them for a minute and then I took them to the kitchen and put them back, making sure each piece went exactly where it had come from.

That night I lay in bed until just after midnight. I got up and went to the medicine cabinet, poured myself a double shot of cough medicine and then crawled back into bed.

For the next week nothing else happened.
Laci didn't say another word about it.
I stayed away from the cough medicine.

Nine days after Laci and Dorito's "intervention" I was in the bedroom.

I heard a noise coming from the kitchen and I walked down the hall to investigate.

Water was pouring full blast from the faucet and both sinks were overflowing. Water flowed in a slow waterfall over the counter and onto the floor.

I shut the water off and sopped up all the water with towels.

Then I went to the Laundromat.

That night I finished off the cough syrup.

Two days later, my phone rang. It was my supervisor, Josef.

"Hi, Josef."

"Hi, David," he said.

"What's up?"

"Well," he said, hesitating, "I wanted to talk to you about Hartman Station."

"Yeah? I sent the stuff up there a few days ago . . . you should have gotten it by now."

"We got it, Dave," he hesitated again. "But there's a problem – the ratios for most of the casings are way off."

"They are?" I asked, wandering over to my desk. I found the Hartman project and tried to find the specification pages.

"And the girder spacing on the portico isn't calculated right."

I found the spec section and started looking at the numbers.

"I'll fix this and send it right away," I told him, although I couldn't remember how to calculate them or imagine how I was possibly going to fix them.

"Dave," Josef was saying, "we'd like to fly you up to Chicago."

"Why?"

"We'd just like to meet with you and talk about what's going on."

"Whatdya mean, *'What's going on'*? Is this a big deal? I just made a few mistakes. I'll fix it and send you what you need this afternoon."

There was no way I could ever have it ready by this afternoon.

"Dave . . ."

"What?"

"Stuff like this has been happening a bit over the past few months. We really need to talk about it."

I sat on the couch, stared at the floor, and waited for Laci. When she walked in the door I looked up at her. She stopped in her tracks and looked back at me. We stared at each other for a long moment.

Finally I nodded at her.

"I'll go," I said.

Made in the USA
Charleston, SC
28 December 2011